A Chicken Was There

TALES OF THE PIONEER CHICKENS WHO HELPED SETTLE THE GREAT AMERICAN WEST

A.A. DAVENPORT

For Jamie...

Contents

Gads Hill, Missouri 1874

I probably shouldn't say I met Jesse James. I didn't actually meet him. In truth, he kicked me for being a distraction to him while he was robbing a train. So, maybe I can say I met his foot, or maybe his boot. But still, how many chickens can say Jesse James kicked them?

I bet you're wondering what I was doing on that train in the first place since chickens don't generally go riding around on trains. Well, the mister who takes care of me fancies himself a chicken expert and has several first-place ribbons from the Boston poultry shows to prove it. When he came west, he waited to get settled before he sent word back east that we were to be shipped out to him so he could start up his prize-winning ways in the West. Most folks in the West don't have fancy purebred chickens like us. We're famous for laying a large number of eggs. I say that not to brag, but because it will become important to my story in a bit.

So, we left Boston on the train. It was supposed to just take four days to get to the West Coast, but let me tell you, it was a lot longer than that. The problem with trains is that they don't just go from one place to another. They have to stop eight million times on the way. It's a wonder anyone actually lives long enough to get to their destination. It seemed like we were lost a lot of the time, they kept taking us off one train and loading us onto another train.

I don't think anyone really knows where all these trains are going. If you get to where you are going, it's what they call a miracle. Anyways, there was always a porter who was supposed to look after us, but to tell you the truth, those porters were pretty bad at their jobs because the longer we traveled, the worse we started to smell. They made sure we had food and water, but no one bothered to clean our crate and no one collected the eggs, so it started to get crowded in there. Oh, I forgot to tell you it was me and three other hens in one crate, and a rooster in his own separate crate. The rooster got his own crate because he can't behave himself. Don't get me started. Back to my story...

We were chugging along when all of a sudden I heard a ruckus and the conductor put the brakes on really fast. Since I was on the wrong end of the crate, everyone else slid over and smashed into me. That wasn't fun because I was sure getting sick of my cratemates. That's when I started to hear shooting and horses galloping around. As soon as the train came to a stop, some misters with hoods over their faces got on and stomped into our car. We were traveling with the luggage and the mail and a giant black box they called a safe. Those misters weren't much interested in anything other than that safe.

That's a good thing because if they knew we were prize winners from Boston, they might have stolen us too. Everyone knows prize-winning chickens are worth a ton. While two of the masked misters used a giant hammer to pound on that safe, the other misters started walking through the cars talking to the passengers on board (none of them, I'm sure, were prize winners). I could hear what they were saying, and they were asking those folks to give them money.

They were much politer than I thought robbers would be. They said nice things to the ladies and promised they wouldn't hurt any of them. That made me feel less stressed, so that's probably why I chose that moment to relieve myself. Since I was shoved by the other girls to the side of the crate, all I could do was squirt through the slats out onto the floor. It landed not very far from one of the robber's boots. He wasn't happy about that. He looked at it and said some cuss words that were totally unnecessary since what happened was nothing but a natural function. No reason to make a fuss about it. Last time I checked, everyone does it. Right then, they finally got that safe open, and the other mister bumped into the cussing mister and made him step in my natural function, which really made him cuss. That's when he kicked the crate.

Now kicking a crate full of chickens who have been cooped up together for days is not a good idea. It startled us so much that we all jumped up and started flapping and trying to shove ourselves to the other side of the crate. All that ruckus got the rooster fussing and cackling in his crate, which just stressed us out even more.

While we were jumping around, we couldn't help cracking all those eggs we had laid. The cracked eggs mixed in with a week's worth of natural functions, and well, it was like a river flowing out of that crate. That's when the mister stepped in it again and this time he slipped and fell right on his backside.

This is important because the other mister yelled out, "Jesse,

3

are you OK?"

That's when I knew that it was the famous train robber Jesse James laying there with raw egg and natural function smeared all over himself. He yelled a string of cuss words that I'm sure they could hear all the way back in Boston and things might have gone badly for us if he hadn't already emptied his six-shooter into the air when he was riding in circles around the train. Before he could get some other ideas for dealing with us, the other mister distracted him by handing him money to put in his saddle bag. It didn't take them long because, I heard later, there sure wasn't a whole lot of money in that safe. Not at all what they had been expecting. By now the other misters were itching to get going, so they all leaped off that train, jumped on their horses, and off they went.

Soon after that, our train headed out and yes, we did eventually make it to our mister who wasn't happy at all to see the mess we were in. We were covered with dried egg mess, and believe me, it isn't easy to get dried egg out of feathers. We lost quite a few feathers when our mister tried to clean us up. No poultry shows for us for a while.

I did my best to keep up with the happenings of the James gang. It wasn't hard since all the newspapers were always telling tales about them and how they robbed from the rich and gave to the poor. In the beginning, some folks even saw them as heroes. But I knew better. I remembered their short tempers and that mean look in their eyes. It wasn't long before some of the shine wore off those boys because, for all of their polite ways, they were after all nothing more than robbers and murderers.

It just took some folks time to start seeing them that way. It reminded me of this hen I once knew. Folks were always praising her for laying double-yolked eggs. I guess having more than one yolk was good eating for some folks. But even though a double-yolked egg might taste good, it will never hatch. So I guess some things that are good in one way are bad in another. That's what that James gang was. Interesting to read about, but underneath all that shine was nothing more than some mean boys who did mean things.

My feathers have started to grow out a bit, but it doesn't matter all that much. There aren't a lot of poultry shows out here in the West. Folks are too busy just trying to make this place a home to care much about blue ribbons. That's OK with me. Blue ribbons aren't all that they're cracked up to be anyways.

Dodge City, Kansas 1881

I heard someone say the other day, "Living in Dodge City is not for chickens."

That bothers me because I don't understand why folks think chickens are cowards. Chickens are some of the bravest creatures walking the planet. I mean, think about it. We have a ton of predators and no defenses. We don't have teeth to bite back, and we can't fly away if someone comes after us. Yet, we go wandering around all day, living our best chicken lives, and not worrying about things we can't help. I call that brave. I have lived in Dodge City all my life, and I'm no coward.

It was a typical spring day in Dodge, and when I say typical, I mean dusty. Dodge is always dusty. There are always so many folks coming and going on horses, in wagons, driving herds of cattle, or just plain old walking. The dust is stirred up all the time, but I don't mind it. I'm used to it. I spend my days with the other chickens scratching around and staying out of folks' way. The number one rule for us chickens is to stay off the boardwalks. If someone catches us on the boardwalk, we will get a swift kick or two. They like to keep the boardwalks clean for the ladies, and when us chickens make a mess, it isn't pleasant for the ladies. Sometimes the hems of their dresses drag through it, and, well, no one wants to see that. So we stay off the boardwalks, and do our scratching in the dirt.

My favorite place to scratch around is at the train depot. When the train comes in lots of folks tend to toss their leftover train snacks on the ground. Let me tell you, there's nothing better than train snacks. You never know what you're going to get. Gingerbread and crackers are two of my favorites, but I'll never turn down sandwich crusts or skillet biscuits. Skillet biscuits with jam are particularly good. One time someone dropped a half-eaten burrito, and I chowed down on that. It was pretty spicy, but I enjoyed it. It did bother my stomach though. A bit later I made a mess that would have ruined ten skirts if I had done it on the boardwalk, but it was all worth it. That burrito was so good!

Back to my story. When I heard the train whistle, I hustled over there quick. Being one of the first there is always important if you want to have your pick of the best snacks. When the train came to a stop, I was happy to see a friend of mine get off. His name was Bat Masterson, and he used to be our sheriff. He was pretty popular here in Dodge, even though he'd been away for some time. I call him a friend because one time I chased a grasshopper up onto the boardwalk, and instead of kicking me, Sheriff Bat just gently nudged me with the toe of his boot off the boardwalk. That's the kind of man he was.

Though I was excited to see Sheriff Bat get off the train, I noticed right away that his face looked grumpy. I wondered if he had eaten one of those spicy burritos and maybe his stomach was bothering him, but in practically no time at all I heard him call out to two misters who were standing around outside the depot office.

Without even a "hello, how are you?" those two misters took off running and hid behind the depot. The next thing I knew, bullets were flying! I let out a squawk and high-tailed it down the street a ways. I wasn't the only one who was dashing around. Folks were running everywhere! In two shakes of a burro's tail, bullets were flying from all directions.

I don't know why the whole town thought this was a good time for a town-wide gunfight, but they did. Folks started shooting from all over the place. When the hitching post I was standing next to got hit and splintered into a million pieces, I panicked, jumped up on the boardwalk, and ran like crazy into the first building I saw. It happened to be the Long Branch Saloon. I skidded to a stop behind the bar and came face to face with old Milt, the bartender. He was on the floor at eye level with me, and he looked as scared as I felt.

Just then, a bullet crashed through the window, shattered the mirror over the bar, and smashed some bottles to boot. I didn't know what was in those bottles at the time, but I know now. It was whiskey. It started running off the bar like a whiskey waterfall. Now, I don't know what it is about running water that gets chickens distracted, but I swear if I see a trickle of water, I can't help myself. I have to investigate and take a drink. So, in the midst of that epic gun battle, that's exactly what I did. I saw that liquid running across the floorboards, so I chased it and dipped my beak in for a drink.

Well, I have to tell you, that was the worst-tasting stuff I have ever tasted! Even worse than the time I was in a hurry and took a drink out of a yellow puddle! Tasting that whiskey made me realize why all the misters in Dodge City were always shooting the place up. If all they drank was whiskey, no wonder they were always out to kill each other! They should just drink water, like us chickens. Chickens understand the importance of hydration.

By this time, the shooting had died down, so Milt and I peeked out from behind the bar. We could see under the saloon's swinging doors, and we saw that one of those two men who had run from Sheriff Bat was in the dirt bleeding. The other one had jumped on a horse and was riding full speed away. I guess he figured rightly that it was time to get out of Dodge.

I heard later that the whole thing started because someone had threatened Sheriff Bat's brother. So, Sheriff Bat came back to Dodge from miles away to make sure his brother wouldn't get bushwhacked. Bushwhacked is when you're minding your own business, just living your life, and someone comes after you, and bam! You're dead. Chickens get bushwhacked all the time. Sheriff Bat just couldn't let anyone do that to his brother, so he put a stop to it. Chickens don't have brothers, but if we did, I sure wouldn't let anyone bushwhack a brother of mine if I could help it.

Sheriff Bat didn't have to go to jail for his part in that town gun-fight, and that man who got shot recovered from his wound. I guess you could say all's well that ends well. I was hoping Sheriff Bat would stick around for a while, but he didn't. Some folks thought he was wrong to come back and stir up trouble like that, but I think that even the most level-headed person can get into trouble if you push him too far.

As for me, I've decided to live a clean life, which means I intend to stay off the boardwalks and stay away from the hard liquor. And those two things should keep me out of trouble. At least I hope so...

Deadwood, Dakota Territory, 1877

Last spring, I met a hen who was traveling on a wagon train from the east, and she told me a story I had a hard time believing. She said in the east, if you stay up until the sun just starts to go down, you can see these special flying bugs she called "light-up bugs." One second they're dark, the next second they light up like a lantern. They blink off and on and if you're quick enough, you can snatch one right out of the air for a bedtime snack. That sounded to me like she was spinning tales because I have seen my share of bugs in my day and not a one of them ever lit up like a lantern. But it made me start thinking about things. I wonder if it's true that something can be dark one second, and light the next.

I live in Deadwood, a town in the Dakota Territory. You might have heard how wild this town is, we have quite a reputation. I suppose Deadwood can be a dangerous place for folks, but not for us chickens. Chickens are too important here in town to be in much danger. Folks take good care of us. The same goes for the pigs. That's because folks here sure like to have breakfast and they need eggs and bacon to make that happen. Eggs come from chickens and bacon comes from pigs. I'm not sure, but I think pigs lay bacon the way chickens lay eggs. At any rate, no one would ever purposely hurt one of us on account of how much folks like to have a good breakfast. Still, I head for the hills when the bullets start flying.

Some folks say Deadwood is a wicked town on account of this fellow named Devil. Folks are always saying that "the devil made me do it" or "that place is full of the devil." It seems to me if someone would just hogtie this devil fellow and send him on the next stagecoach out of here, this would be a more peaceful town. But no one ever suggests that. Maybe this devil guy is just the poor lunk that everyone blames all the trouble on. Sometimes it's convenient to have someone else to blame for your own wrongdoing.

One person folks like to blame for our town's rowdy reputation is a missus named Calamity Jane. You always know when Calamity Jane is around because she likes to holler at everyone she sees. One time, me and some other hens were out scratching around in front of the blacksmith's stable when Calamity Jane came riding down the street hollerin' about her horse needing shoes. When I heard her, I knew that Calamity was in one of her moods she gets in when she's spent too much time in the saloon. I've seen plenty of horses in my life, and everyone knows they don't wear shoes.

Well, right about when she got to us, she stopped her horse. When she tried to get down, she lost her balance, fell off the horse, and landed in a mud puddle! Mud went flying everywhere! Us chickens didn't appreciate it since we like to look our best and keep our feathers clean and shiny. Now we were all splattered with mud. But I don't think Calamity got hurt because she started giggling. Then, she started cussin' something awful when folks just pointed and laughed at her instead of helping her out of that puddle.

That's how it was most of the time with Calamity Jane. Folks liked her because she was loud and didn't act like you expected her to. But then, folks were mean to her too. They would make fun of her because she dressed like a mister when she was really a missus. Most of the respectable dressed ladies in our town wouldn't talk to her at all, and some even crossed to the other side of the street when they saw her coming because they didn't approve of her ways. She always acted like she didn't care about how folks treated her, but I know different.

One day the pox flew into town, and folks started getting sick right and left. A lot of folks even died. I didn't think much about it until my missus got the pox, and she was so sick in bed that she forgot to feed us. You might wonder why we didn't just eat some bugs if we didn't have anything else to eat, but remember how I told you that Deadwood was a dangerous place? Well, it was so dangerous that not even the bugs would come into town, so us chickens were gettin' pretty hungry. We didn't have to worry long though, because Calamity Jane showed up at our house and marched right in to nurse my missus back to health.

This was a puzzlement to me since my missus was one of those respectable dressed ladies who thought Calamity Jane was a nuisance. But Calamity didn't care. She nursed her anyway. When she went to leave, you would think that she wouldn't pay us any mind on account of how many sick folks there were around town who needed tending, but before she left our place she stopped by the shed and filled up our pan with cracked corn. That's how I know that even though she was good at cussin' and pretendin' to be ornery, Calamity Jane had a good heart.

Our missus wasn't the only sick one Calamity Jane got to helpin'. There were so many who got the pox that they began hauling sick folks into these special tents to keep them all together. Most of the well folks were so scared the pox was going to get them that they didn't lift a finger to help. Well, that Calamity Jane stared that pox down and went into those tents and nursed folks back to health. Some say she saved their lives and some even called her an angel. I'm not sure what an angel is, but the folks who said it were so respectful when they spoke that I guess an angel is a pretty good thing to be. You know, the respectable dressed ladies of the town were so scared the pox would get them that they never left their houses and let Calamity do all the nursing. So I guess Calamity proved to that whole town who was respectable and who wasn't.

I guess things would have continued on pretty much the same for Calamity if it wasn't for what happened to her friend, Wild Bill Hickock. One day he was playing cards in a saloon and someone came up behind him and shot him for no good reason at all. That's when our town decided to get our very first sheriff. Being a sheriff is a lot like being a rooster. You're in charge of making sure that everyone behaves themselves. You would think that a town with a reputation for being bad wouldn't want someone to make them be good, but you'd be wrong about that. We had to get a sheriff because a lot of folks around here like to play cards, and they didn't want to get shot while playing like Mister Wild Bill did.

The man they got to be our sheriff was named Mister Bullock. Since we have gun fights almost every day here in Deadwood, Sheriff Bullock probably thought he would have to do a lot of gunslinging to get folks under control, but that wasn't the case. I guess everyone just got tired of being bad and decided to behave themselves, so the sheriff whipped this town into shape without even firing a shot! I guess that means being bad is more like a choice than something that you were just born being.

Eventually, they caught that mister who shot Wild Bill. I was hoping that would make Calamity feel better, but most folks said she got even wilder. I don't know about that, but I remember one day when we were scratching around down by the burial ground Calamity Jane was there by his grave, and she had tears running down her face. Crying isn't something that chickens do, so I don't know what it feels like, but I hope it made Calamity feel better to do it.

So now that we have a sheriff, Deadwood's become a more peaceful town and I'm not sorry for that. Sometimes, I think Deadwood is a bit like that light-up bug, the one that can be light one second and dark the next. Or maybe there's no such thing as light-up bugs and that hen from the east was just pulling my leg and laughing at me for believing her story in the first place. Maybe things have to be one or the other, and can't have both light and dark in them at the same time. I don't know if that bug is real or not, but before I close my eyes tonight I'm going to have a look out the coop window at Deadwood as it gets dark. Who knows? Maybe I'll see one.

Denver, Colorado 1886

I joined Buffalo Bill's Wild West Show quite by accident. In case you don't know what a Wild West Show is, it's when folks pay money to go and watch other folks pretend that things are happening when they really aren't. I don't know how folks have the time to watch all that pretending, but they do. Us chickens are too busy for such things.

It was when the show spent the winter in New Orleans that I joined them. There were several hundred folks involved in the show, so as you can imagine, it took a lot of food to feed so many. The farmer who raised me gathered me and about fifty other young roosters into large crates and sold us to the show. They stacked our crates outside a covered wagon called the chuckwagon. Then, a man reached into a crate, grabbed one of us, and took him behind the chuckwagon. After that, all I heard was a *squawk* and a *thwack*, then silence. Then, a cloud of feathers came floating out from behind the chuckwagon.

I sure didn't know what was going on behind that wagon, and I was not itching to find out! The next time that man opened the crate to reach in and grab one of us, I jumped with all my might. I flapped my wings and squawked as loud as I could. I startled that man so much that he knocked the whole crate over and roosters went flap-running everywhere! I went flapping my wings, squawking, and running full speed through the camp. Folks came out of their tents to laugh and some joined in the chase.

I soon found myself being chased by five or six misters until I was cornered. I was surrounded by canvas tents with no space between them to slip out. I panicked, made a mighty jump, and flapped my wings as hard as I could. I was hopeful I could fly over the tents, but they were too high and just as I was about to slam into the side of a tent, it opened and I flew right into that tent!

The missus who opened the tent to see what the ruckus was screamed as I flew right past her and landed in the corner by her cot. One of the misters who had been chasing me stepped up and said he would go in and get me.

But she said, "No. The poor thing is scared to death. Let me get him."

I was huddled in a corner too scared and too exhausted to do much but sit there, panting. I let her pick me up because she was talking to me softly, and I needed a little kindness. She took a half-eaten strawberry from a plate near her bed and offered it to me. I know I should have been suspicious, but it smelled so good I couldn't resist. This made her laugh. She declared that she would keep me and train me and I would become a part of her act.

My missus was true to her word, and she trained me to perform with her on her horse. At first, I wanted no part of that horse, but she started getting me used to it slowly. She'd take me for short rides around the ring, stroke my neck, and talk to me the whole time so I knew I had nothing to be scared of. Soon, she fashioned a strap behind the saddle and hooked my feet into it so I couldn't move. Then, she taught me to ride back there.

It was scary at first, but I learned that if I squatted down and half opened my wings I could keep my balance no matter how fast the horse was going. While I was riding behind her, she would do all sorts of crazy things, like slide out of the saddle until she was upside down and her head was almost bouncing off the ground. Sometimes, she would stand up on top of the saddle while the horse was galloping full speed, and sometimes, she would even stand on her hands. The audience would clap and holler like crazy when she did those tricks. I did my part by crowing up a storm the whole time we were galloping around the ring. Sometimes I wonder why my missus agreed to do all those crazy tricks. I guess some folks just don't have a lot of sense sometimes.

It wasn't long before the missus and I were stars. Some would say we were even more popular than Annie Oakley. All she knew how to do was shoot a gun. Anyone can do that! What the missus and I did took real talent. I got to where I enjoyed being in the show. One of the best times for me was when I got my nickname, "Little Chief." That name was given to me by none other than Sitting Bull himself. Sitting Bull was an Indian, he got special permission to leave his reservation and join our show.

A reservation is a place for the Indians to live. It's like a fenced-in chicken yard. Before I was a popular performer in the Buffalo Bill Show, I lived in a chicken yard. It keeps you safe but sometimes it can be hard if you see a nice beetle walking just outside the fence and you can't get it if you want to.

Well, back to how I got my nickname, one early morning I was scratching around on the side of our tent. The missus used to leave the door to my crate unfastened since I liked to get up when the sun got up and most of the show folk slept late. As I was scratching I noticed a man who was sneaking around. I didn't like the looks of him. Chickens never sneak. We have nothing to hide. This man was definitely sneaking. I kept scratching around, but I kept one eye on him. He came up to the tent and whispered my missus' name through the flap. When she didn't answer, he untied one of the strings, bent down low, and stuck his whole head in the flap.

Now, one thing chickens know is who belongs in the coop and who doesn't. Back in the day when I was a real chicken instead of a show chicken, a possum came into our coop one night, and we sure put up a fuss about it. Everyone knows that possums aren't welcome. When that man stuck his head in my missus' tent, he was just like that possum, and I had a duty to protect my missus.

I jumped up and let out a huge squawk. Since he was bent double, I used my spurs to spear him right on his rear end. He yelped in surprise, then lost his balance, and fell over backward. He landed on his back end and was sitting up straight in the mud. That's when I struck again. This time I aimed for his head, but he shielded his face with his arm and let out a high-pitched scream like the little girls in the crowd would do when the show reenacted Custer's Last Stand.

Then he hauled himself out of the mud and took off running. I chased him all through the camp. He was slip-sliding in the mud most of the time, and every time he went down I spurred him as hard as I could. That man yelped so loud he woke up the whole camp. When we passed through the Indian section of the camp, the Indians thought we were the funniest thing ever. Finally, that sneaker jumped up into the chuck wagon, and that's when I had to give up the pursuit. I wanted no part of the chuckwagon, but I did let out a crow or two just to let that man know who was the boss.

As I strutted back to the missus, folks clapped for me. That's when Sitting Bull declared that from now on my new name was Little Chief. They even made a poster to put all over town with a picture of my missus and me.

Chickens can't read, but I heard from folks around camp that the poster said, "Little Chief, the Bravest Chicken in the Whole Wild West".

I sure was proud. I heard later that Buffalo Bill fired that man who tried to visit my missus in her tent. Sneaking was not allowed at Buffalo Bill's Wild West Show.

That was more than a year ago now, and we continue to travel everywhere performing our show. Sitting Bull isn't with us anymore. He went home to his reservation. He was killed when some folks decided he might cause trouble. I don't think someone should be killed when they haven't done anything wrong. How can we ever know for sure what someone else *might* do?

The reservation was supposed to be a safe place for Sitting Bull to live. He'd have been safer if he just lived in a town or on a farm like other folks. Plenty of chickens live together with ducks, geese, turkeys, and guineas. Just about anything with feathers can live together. If feathered things can all live together peaceably, why can't folks?

I once knew a hen who waited until she had as many eggs as she could fit under her, then she settled in to hatch them. Hens aren't particular about whose eggs they sit on. When they get the urge to hatch, they pretty much go all in. Eventually, she hatched nine pretty chicks, but she kept sitting. Sometimes a hen just knows that another egg will hatch. A few days later, she hatched one more, but it wasn't a chick, it was a duck!

Well, she raised that little duck along with the rest of her chicks. When she was out in the yard teaching them to scratch, the duck couldn't scratch. His little feet weren't made for that. Every time the whole group passed by a puddle, that duck would get in and swim around. The chicks couldn't do that because their little feet weren't made to swim. But at the end of the day, they would all gather together under the warmth of their mother and sleep and be happy. So, I never understood why the white folks made the Indians live fenced-in when their feet weren't made to stay in one place. I've seen a lot of this country in my travels, and it seems to me that there's room for everyone to live together and be happy. At least that's how I see it.

Tombstone, Arizona Territory, 1881

I have a cross-beak. It's something that I've had since I was hatched. It means my beak doesn't close right. I've heard some folks say my beak looks like a pair of scissors, whatever that is. Most chickens born with a cross beak don't survive very long because they can't get enough food in them to stay healthy. I remember when I was young, I was powerful hungry all the time. Then one day, I was pecking at some table scraps and got distracted by something mid-peck, so I turned my head suddenly and kind of scooped that scrap of food right into my mouth.

That's when I discovered that I could eat better if I would scoop instead of peck. I've been scooping ever since. I guess there's a solution for most things that ail you. It's not a perfect solution. I'm still smaller than the other hens, but I get by and manage to lay an egg most days, so I guess I can't complain.

I've been living here in Tombstone since I was hatched a couple of years ago. Folks say that Tombstone is a modern town based on the fact that we have an opera house. I once wandered by the opera house and heard the most awful noise coming out of there. It sounded like a goose getting her tail feathers pulled out. If all that screeching means we're modern, then I don't much want to be modern.

My missus runs a boarding house here in town. That's a place for folks to come and sleep if they don't have anywhere else to sleep. I think it's generous of the missus to invite folks in. Us chickens definitely don't like strangers in our hen house. If we get a new hen and she puts her in there with us, we make sure to peck her and let her know we were there first.

Since folks are always coming and going at the boarding house, I've had the chance to meet a lot of interesting people. One time, a man came out the back door to smoke. Smoking is when folks put a stick in their mouth, light it on fire, and swallow the smoke. It doesn't look tasty. While he was smoking, he noticed me trying to scoop up some ants from an ant hill on the side of the porch steps.

I heard him say, "Tarnation! What's wrong with that bird's face?"

My missus explained to him that I was born with a cross beak and I had to struggle to get food every day. She said maybe it was time she put me out of my misery and put me in the pot to stew. I'm not sure what stewing is, and I don't think I want to find out. That man bent down and got a closer look at my beak. After he thought for a minute, he told her to just let me be because sometimes folks have to deal with things that come on them through no fault of their own. They shouldn't be treated badly for it. I guess that man saved my life that day.

His name was Doc Holiday, though I don't know why people called him that. The only thing he knew how to doctor was teeth, and judging by how many teeth folks were missing in our town, teeth doctors must not be very good at their jobs. I think Doc Holiday understood about me because I heard that when he was young, he was tending to his sick Ma, and that sickness jumped straight out of her and landed inside of him. That's why he coughed so much. He knew what it was like to have to deal with hardships that came through no fault of his own.

My life here in Tombstone is pretty much the same every day. There aren't a lot of bugs to eat. Since this is a big city, what this town lacks in bugs it makes up for in garbage. We spend our days picking through the garbage piles in back of the stores and other buildings. My favorite place to pick through the garbage is the Oriental Saloon. They have the best garbage by far. There's another saloon called The Birdcage Saloon, and at first, I thought that would be an ideal place to look for treats. But it's nowhere close to having the good eats we get at the Oriental.

When we aren't pecking around for food, we often enjoy a relaxing dust bath, since dust is in no short supply around these parts. When us chickens take a dust bath, we find a little hollow in the dirt, settle in, and use our wings to toss the dirt all over us. Then, when we stand up and shake off, we come up clean! I guess you could say we get clean by getting dirty.

One time I flew up on a hitching post and looked in the missus' window and she was in there taking a dust bath, but get this, instead of using dust, she was sitting in a tub of water! She was splashing that water all over herself. Can you imagine that? Some folks don't have the good sense God gave them. So between garbage picking and dust baths, life is pretty good.

The only thing we really have to be on the lookout for is little boys with slingshots. You may think it's no big deal to get beaned with a rock from a slingshot but you would be wrong! It hurts. A lot. I once overheard the missus reading a story from a big book to her daughter about a boy who killed a giant man with just a rock from his slingshot. Well, that made me even more determined to stay away from boys and their slingshots.

One day we had some excitement in town. A couple of hens and I were enjoying the garbage at the back of the general store when we heard some loud voices down by the corral. I had just stumbled on some spoiled cabbage when I heard gunshots. Guns are a type of slingshot. Just louder. Some men were down by the horse corral, and they were slinging rocks at each other out of their guns all at once. It didn't last long, but when it was over, three of them were dead!

I'm not sure what made them all so angry that they decided to slingshot each other to death like that. It made me think of a time I chased a June bug clear down the street almost to the blacksmith's shop. Just when I finally caught it, another hen came up from behind and stole that June bug right out of my mouth. If you think I was mad about that, you're right!

That night I made sure I didn't sleep next to that hen on the roost. But you know something? When I woke up in the morning I wasn't that angry anymore. And after a great breakfast of stale cornbread and leftover mashed potatoes that I found in the back of the Oriental Saloon, I was even less angry. Then, that afternoon as I was taking my dust bath, I remembered a time when I swiped a grasshopper right out of the mouth of another hen, and I began to realize that I shouldn't have been mad about that June bug when I done the same thing myself before. Maybe those men didn't have to die that fine morning. Maybe a good night's sleep, a satisfying meal, and a relaxing dust bath could have changed all that happened that day. They just needed to take a moment to think things through. Or maybe human folks have more important things to be angry about than stolen June bugs. What do I know? After all, I'm just a chicken.

Chisholm Trail, Indian Territory, 1870

V ery few chickens can say they traveled on an honest-to-good-ness cattle drive, but I did, and let me tell you, it was quite an adventure!

We left San Antonio on an early spring day. We were herding several thousand Texas Longhorns along with us. I rode in a crate strapped to the back of the chuckwagon along with three other hens. Now, as I mentioned, chickens on a cattle drive were unusual because they aren't the most practical thing to bring along. But Cookie (that's what the men called our chuckwagon cook) got the notion that if we each laid one egg a day, every four or five days he would have enough eggs for the boys to have scrambled eggs to go along with their frijoles.

I guess he figured that if we weren't good travelers he could always serve us up next to the frijoles. Cookie took a mighty pride in his cooking. What he lacked in kindness and patience, he made up for in some of the best grub the territory had ever seen. Our trail boss used to say he had boys lined up begging to ride for him just to get a taste of Cookie's grub! I don't know if all that is true, but that's what I heard.

For the first couple of weeks, I worried that my days on the trail might be shorter than I anticipated. You see, chickens don't lay eggs well if we're stressed or out of our usual surroundings. Between the four of us, we were barely putting out an egg a day while we were still getting used to life on the prairie. Cookie wasn't happy about it, and he cussed us something awful and threatened to fry us up for dinner if we didn't start producing eggs regular.

Most of the trail cooks used sourdough to make their biscuits. That way, they wouldn't need eggs. But Cookie hated sourdough with a passion, and he wanted to serve the men real biscuits made with eggs and flour. Not "sinkers," which is what he used to call sourdough biscuits with a snarl in his voice. Cookie sure was grumpy. I guess the start of a long trail ride can be difficult for folks and chickens alike.

Cookie wasn't the only one who was edgy. The Longhorns were having a tough time adjusting to trail life as well. Even though they weren't expected to lay eggs, they were expected to move along in an orderly fashion. While they were learning to do that, they were jumpy and skittish. The cowboys were constantly worried about stampedes. I found out why when that's exactly what those cows did one stormy night.

We were only a couple of weeks into the trip when the air started to rumble something fierce and the lightning lit up the night like it was noontime. We were asleep in our crate under the chuckwagon when it all started, and to tell you the truth, we would have slept through it all if not for the ground shaking. When chickens are asleep we're dead to the world, and nothing can wake us. At least that's what I thought.

Then I felt the ground pounding under my feet and the chuck-wagon above us started bouncing around. I opened my eyes and saw Cookie. He was dressed only in his bright red long johns, boots, and hat and trying to hitch up the mules to the chuckwagon so he could get us out of there. But that was taking too long, so he ended up giving up on that idea and started jumping around, shouting, and waving his hat to try and steer the cows away from us. From where I was huddled under the wagon I could see what seemed like millions of cow legs stomping down the dust and coming straight for us as the lightning flashed through the sky. I thought we were goners for sure until I saw cowboys on horses racing around from the side, cutting the cows off and steering them away from us. It was close, but we survived.

For the next few days, we didn't travel the trail. The boys were busy out trying to round up the cows who had run away from the herd. So, myself and the other hens got to explore the grass and eat our fill of beetles and caterpillars. We were doing better with egg production, so Cookie stopped threatening us and started to use his skills, and our eggs, to make the boys some pancakes and cobblers, which they appreciated since they were so tired from searching everywhere for runaway cows.

I liked the cowboys for the most part. They would throw us crusts from their bread and other bits they were through with. I think they liked seeing us scratch around because we reminded them of home. Only one of the cowboys gave me a problem. His name was Stinky, and I can only imagine why they called him that. He used to chunk rocks at me and complain loudly to Cookie about how a fried chicken drummy would taste real good right about now.

It made me nervous that he was so popular with everyone. He liked to tell stories and jokes, and I even caught Cookie with a slight smile on his face at one of Stinky's impossible tales. I got a bit worried that Cookie would start to take Stinky's suggestion about fried chicken drummies seriously, and then I wouldn't live to see Abilene at all. I really wanted to see Abilene. Folks said it was a "cow town," and I had never seen cows in charge of a town before.

But as it turned out, I didn't have to worry too much about Stinky. After I saved his life, he stopped yammering about fried chicken...

It was pretty early in the morning and Stinky had ridden a double watch the night before. One of the boys was feeling poorly, and Stinky volunteered to ride his watch. He crawled out of his bedroll and stumbled over to get his coffee at the chuckwagon, then sat down on an old hollow log to wait for breakfast. Cookie growled at him because he didn't like the boys to show up unwashed and wearing nothing but their boots and long underwear, but Stinky was too tired to care.

I was out scratching around and enjoying the beautiful morning when I noticed some movement in the grass. Thinking it was a centipede or a small lizard, I ducked my head down low and started chasing it. I was concentrating so hard on the chase that I didn't notice that I chased it right up to that hollow log where Stinky was sitting. It was then that I noticed it was a small snake. Now small snakes are no problem at all. Us chickens can spend all day picking one apart. After all, who doesn't enjoy a tasty snake dinner?

But to my surprise, the snake turned around and snipped at me. I jumped back in time so it missed me, but it startled me so much that I started putting up a fuss. Chickens fuss about all sorts of things. Being startled will definitely get us going. Well, Stinky was in no mood for my noise, and he took off his hat and used it to try and swat me. That's when we heard it. A loud, clear rattling sound. Now, I didn't know that sound but Stinky sure did. He shrieked, went pale, and popped up off that log like a grasshopper popping up half a second before a beak snaps it up. No one could ever say Stinky was a coward. I watched him volunteer to be first across the Red River to try and find us a way over. When his horse stepped in a hole and they both went completely under, he came back up a few yards downstream with a huge smile on his face, clutching his hat in one hand and the reins in the other and whooping a rebel yell. Stinky was no scaredy cat, but that tiny snake put a look of fear on his face like I'd never seen before.

One of the boys emptied his six shooter all over that snake, which was a shame because after that there wasn't much left of it to eat. But to my surprise, the whole camp started talking about how I had saved Stinky's life! Truth be told by chasing that snake, I was just trying to secure a snack, It wasn't my intention to save anyone's life. Certainly not Stinky's. But I did enjoy all the attention the boys flung at me and I enjoyed the bits of dried apple cobbler and boiled potatoes that the whole camp saw fit to toss in my direction at supper that night. Even Stinky tossed a bit of steak at me, though he didn't look in my direction when he did it.

When we went to sleep that night, my belly was full and my heart was fuller. I began to think that because of that snake, I might get to see the cow town after all. As I closed my eyes I dozed off to the rustle of the breeze through my feathers, and the distant sound of cows mooing while cowboys sang them to sleep. Maybe being a trail herd chicken isn't such a bad thing after all.

Fort Leavenworth, Kansas 1878

I am a part of the Nez Perce Indian tribe. A tribe is kind of like a flock, but not really. A flock is a group of chickens who share the same ways. A tribe is a group of folks who share the same ways AND have the same heart. I haven't always been a Nez Perce. They adopted me when my folks traded me for a hand-woven basket. They only agreed to the trade because the Indian missus who made the basket said that Chief Joseph was the one to make it. I don't think that was true because in all the months I have lived here, I have never seen Chief Joseph making baskets.

We live here at Fort Leavenworth because we are prisoners of war. I know about war because where I used to live we had two roosters that were always fighting with each other to see who was the best. But the war Chief Joseph fought wasn't to try and be better than anyone else. He fought a war so he could take all his folks back to the land that was stolen from them.

I don't understand why folks would steal their land. Here at Fort Leavenworth, there is empty land as far as my eyes can see. Why couldn't folks just come and live on this land and let the Nez Perce stay where they have lived for years and years?

I remember a time when my old missus brought us chickens a whole plate full of burnt biscuits to eat. You may think burnt biscuits aren't good eating, but they are. They're only burnt on the outside. You have to be patient and peck away the burnt part to get to the fluffy biscuit underneath. The hen that got to them first snapped one up and took off with it. Even though there were enough biscuits for everyone to have their own, we all chased after her and tried to steal hers right out of her mouth. Maybe that's why Chief Joseph lost his land. He had it first and other folks came along and snapped it away from him instead of getting their own.

Life here at Fort Leavenworth isn't nice for us. We aren't free to go where we want. We have to stay here on an old abandoned, dusty racetrack where there are no trees and no grass. Chief Joseph isn't here with us all the time. He's busy talking to folks and trying to get them to let us go home to the place of our ancestors. Chickens don't have ancestors, but now that I'm a Nez Perce, I do. I think ancestors are important because it makes me feel like I am a part of something that has always been here and always will be here.

Some of the folks say that next year Chief Joseph will go to a far-away place called Washington and talk to the chief of the white men and tell him how much our hearts need to go home. I hope it works, but for now, we do what the soldiers tell us to do and make baskets and necklaces for the white folks to buy from us. They always come around to look at us. All of them want to see our chief. Most folks are interested in our chief, and they think he was brave for fighting a war to get us home.

But some folks don't understand why we need to go home so badly. They think we should just be willing to go anywhere and call it home. We live in a time when folks are moving all over the country and starting over in new places. They don't understand why the Indians can't do the same.

I once heard a story of a lady who wanted to add some peacocks to her flock of chickens. She bought some peacock eggs from a zoo back east and shoved them under a broody hen and one of them hatched. Now peacocks aren't like chickens. They have feathers and beaks like chickens, but their ways are different. When that little peacock grew up, he never felt at home with the chickens. He was always looking around like he was looking for someone. He knew he didn't belong. Then, one day, he left. He just wandered off looking for home. I think the Nez Perce are like that peacock. They need to find their home, and it can't be just anywhere.

Chief Joseph talks a lot about how someday things will be different. He says that a hundred years from now, in our country, no one will care what color your skin is or how different your ways are. All men will be equal. I believe he's right. I just think it will be sooner than a hundred years. Us chickens learned at the beginning that all chickens were the same even though some of us are brown, some are black, and some are white. Folks are every bit as smart as chickens.

We always have soldiers guarding us here at the fort. I'm not sure why. We are too tired and sick to put up a fight, and there is nowhere for us to escape to, except home, and they won't let us go there. Sometimes our guards are soldiers we call buffalo soldiers because their skin is the color of the buffalo. I have heard of the fight that was fought in our country so the buffalo soldiers could be free. The buffalo soldiers were treated badly for being different.

Now they treat us badly. You would think that they would understand us since they once were us, but they don't. One time a chicken in our flock got a cough and before you knew it, all of us were coughing. Maybe bad ways are like that cough. Eventually, everyone catches it.

For now, we stay here in the dust. We are fed by the soldiers, but they look away when they feed us. We are promised that we will go somewhere better soon, but our old ones grumble and say we've been made promises before. Chief Joseph doesn't like the grumbles. He says that if all the earth's children would open their hearts more, we wouldn't have troubles. Chief Joseph wants us to rest and get stronger because we still have a long way to travel to get back home. Most folks are amazed that he still believes he will get home again. I know he believes it because his father's bones are calling to him to go home. Chickens don't have fathers, but if we did, I would want Chief Joseph to be my father.

Chief Joseph is like a rooster who looks you in the eyes and lets you know that he can fight if he has to but believes there's another way. I don't know what the future holds for us. I don't know if I will ever get to see the home that I have heard so much about but never seen for myself. But I will follow my Chief because his heart is strong, and his ways are good. Maybe someday everyone else will know that too.

Angels Camp, California, 1865

I live in a mountain town called Angels Camp. Angels isn't a big town. We only have one street with a few buildings. Most of the folks who live here are miners who live in tents on the sides of the mountains. At night, they all light their lanterns, and it looks like the hillsides are full of stars. I don't live in a tent. I live in a coop with a bunch of other hens behind the best hotel in Angels.

Our job is to provide eggs for the folks who come to stay at the hotel. Most of the folks who come to stay are miners. They spend their days scratching for gold, which is a rock. You can't eat rocks, so I spend my days scratching for bugs, especially snails. I love snails.

The good thing about snails is that not only do they taste good, but some of them have shells and it takes some figuring to get them out of those shells. Chickens aren't lazy, and we don't like to be bored, so when we find a snail, we enjoy pecking away at the shell to get at the snail inside.

One of my favorite snails isn't a snail at all. It's called a banana slug. Slugs don't have shells, but I don't mind because banana slugs are enormous. They aren't hard to spot because they're bright yellow and that makes them stick out a mile away. The only downside is that because it's easy to see them, there's a lot of competition to actually get one, which makes it special when I end up with one. I'm not sure why folks call them "banana" slugs because I don't know what a banana is. Maybe banana is the folks' word for "tasty." That would mean these are really called "tasty slugs," and that fits them just fine.

So, I guess you could say everyone in this town spends their days huntin' around for things. The menfolk search for gold while us chickens search for snails and slugs. All that searching can get boring for the folks, so another thing they like to do is called gambling. Gambling is when folks come to the hotel in the evening carrying a small bag of gold dirt.

Then, they spend the rest of the evening figuring out who will go home with a lot of gold dirt and who will go home with nothing at all. I'm glad chickens don't gamble since we don't have any use for gold. I guess we would have to gamble with banana slugs. If you gamble away a banana slug you worked all day long just to find, that's a rotten shame. And if you win at gambling and end up with a whole bunch of banana slugs, then you have more than you need, and what's the good in that?

One day, last February, a couple of men showed up in Angels to stay at our hotel, and what I remember most about them was that they liked to tell stories. It rained for several weeks straight and those men would sit on the hotel porch and yammer on and on. They made each other laugh and spun tales that none of us could believe. Even though it was raining, us chickens still got out and scratched around because all that rain made the worms come up out of the dirt. Worms are good eating.

We would scoot all over the front lawn of the hotel scratching for worms in the dirt and scooping them up out of puddles. I suppose we must have been pretty entertaining because those men would sit in the rocking chairs and laugh at us. They were probably amused because when chickens get soaking wet we're pretty funny looking. Being wet makes us look skinny and it makes our legs look longer. Chickens are at their best looking when our feathers are dry and fluffy. Well, those men would toss pieces of bread from their sandwiches at us and laugh when we all ran to try and beat each other to the bread. I didn't care that they laughed, worms and bread are as good a meal as a banana slug.

One man in particular was generous with his sandwich. His name was Samuel Clemens, and he loved to write down the stories the other folks would tell. During those wet weeks on the porch, he filled up an entire notebook with stories. One story really got him laughing. It was the story of a man named Jim Smiley who liked to gamble. He would gamble on just about anything.

One day, Mr. Smiley gambled that his chicken could beat another chicken in a race. I wasn't skeptical about that part of the story because chickens are sure fast runners when they want to be. When a grasshopper is hopping by, us chickens definitely race to be the one who will get it. It was the next part of the story that made me roll my eyes.

It seems Mr. Smiley played a trick on someone by fooling his chicken into eating buckshot instead of corn so it was too heavy to race. That's how he was able to win his bet. I was pretty disgusted with that story because no self-respecting chicken would eat buckshot. We're smart enough to know the difference between buckshot and cracked corn. But those folks on the porch sure thought it was the funniest story they had ever heard.

I'm not sure what was funny about it since having a belly full of buckshot must have been painful for the poor chicken. Maybe it was the way he told the story that made it funny. I decided to head to the back of the hotel and scratch for worms back there since I didn't care to hear any more stories that made chickens sound dumb.

Sometime later I heard that Mister Clemens wrote that story down and sold it to a newspaper, but he changed the facts and made it about a frog full of buckshot instead of a chicken. I was happy to hear that since everyone knows that a chicken is way smarter than a frog.

A frog is a lot more likely to swallow a bunch of buckshot. My opinion of Mr. Clemens went back up once I knew he was able to actually write a believable story. I hoped Mr. Clemens would come back someday and share some more of his sandwiches. But to this day I haven't seen hide nor hair of him back in Angels. So instead of bread, I will have to content myself with tasty slugs, and that's OK with me.

Virginia City, Nevada 1876

Virginia City is a town where folks come to get rich. They try to get rich by digging for silver in the mines. But there are plenty of folks who get rich in other ways, like running a store or a restaurant. Some folks even try to get rich by pretending to be something they're not.

One time, my mister had a bad tummy ache and he went to see a doctor. Well, the medicine that doctor gave him made his tummy ache even worse. As it turns out, he wasn't a doctor at all! He was just a pretender. But no one cares about that sort of thing out here. This is a place where folks can try to be something new. Look at me! I used to be a regular, old, boring chicken who did nothing all day but scratch around and lay an egg every now and then, and now I'm a famous trick chicken with a real job! Who would have thought it could happen to someone like me?

Most chickens don't have jobs, but I'm proud to be one of the few who work for a living. My job is very important. My mister and I provide a lot of fun and excitement for folks who are tired from working all day long. We wander around on the streets and invite folks to stop and play a card game with us. The game is called Three

40

Card Monte, and it's pretty simple to play.

Folks bet some money that they can find a certain card. Then, it gets moved around a table really fast, and they have to keep track of it. They have to guess which one is their card. If they guess right, they get more money than they started with. If they guess wrong, they lose their money but gain a smile and a laugh. I don't know why sometimes folks don't smile and laugh at the end of the game. Maybe they don't understand that they're supposed to.

Perhaps you have heard of our game and wonder what my part in it is. Well, let me start with how I met my mister. He picked me up off the streets of the town where I was living a couple of years ago when I was quite literally running for my life. A hungry miner was about to chop my head off and eat me. (I don't think he wanted to eat my head. That's why he was going to chop it off.) I surprised him with my strength, jumped out of his arms, and started flap-running down an alley.

When my mister saw me running and squalling with a dirty, long-bearded miner holding a knife and running after me, he scooped me up, jumped into a half-empty moonshine barrel behind a saloon, and held my beak shut so I wouldn't give us away. Well, that miner ran right past us, and we just barely had enough time to climb out of that barrel before the saloon owner came out and started filling up an empty whiskey bottle with his homemade brew. My mister saved my life that day, and we've been together ever since then.

Soon after he saved me, my mister decided to train me to be a part of his card game. You may think chickens are stupid and can't be trained, but you would be wrong about that. Chickens are very intelligent. We can remember folks, see colors, and recognize voices and words. Of course, it helps that I'm one of the more intelligent chickens you could ever meet.

I learned my part in the game quickly. In Three Card Monte, all the player has to do is pick the right card. My mister thought it would be good to show folks how easy it is to do that, so he taught me to pick the right card. It's pretty easy. I have a perch next to the box where he lays out the cards. When he's ready for me to do some picking, I just hop off and go and peck the right card. How do I know what card to peck? I just peck the card that's closest to where he rests his hand. It's really that simple!

I learned to do it because he would give me a treat if I pecked the right card. A small piece of flapjack was my favorite treat, and he always has a couple of day-old flapjacks in his pockets as a snack for both of us when we get hungry. Nowadays, I peck the right card even if I don't get a treat just because I know I'm supposed to. You may be wondering why the folks playing the game don't figure out how to pick the card closest to his hand.

Well, my mister has two hands and eight fingers. He lost two fingers in a mining accident a few years back. He likes to wave that three-finger hand over the cards right before he asks the player to pick one. Most folks are so distracted by the sight of his mangled hand that they watch it and ignore his other hand, which he rests by the right card for me to see. I don't find a lot of interest in his bad hand. Chickens have accidents all the time and missing a toe or two is no big deal for us.

So, I always pick the right card and folks clap and hurrah for me as my mister explains that if a chicken can do it, surely they can too!

Then, I go back to my perch and let the folks have a try at it.

So that's my job. My mister says I draw customers because they've never seen a chicken who can play Three Card Monte as well as I can. He likes to set up his box near the train depot or the stagecoach office so he can meet new folks coming into town and see if they want to play. He says folks coming in on the train or the stage are from the east and aren't used to seeing three-fingered men and smart chickens, so they will be more likely to enjoy our game.

We have to be very careful though, we tend to draw a crowd and a crowd draws lawmen. For some reason, lawmen aren't impressed with us and the way we make our living. We've been thrown out of a town or two by deputies who are jealous of all the happiness we bring to people. Sometimes it's not just lawmen who get jealous. There have been times when other folks have come after us too.

My mister and I sleep with our mule Sally in the stable, and one time, while we were visiting Carson City, we had to skedaddle out of town in the middle of the night when some folks came into the stable with a bucket of tar. They said they would take the feathers off of me and use them to tar and feather my mister! Well, my mister didn't want to get sticky, and I didn't want to be naked, so that's when we knew it was time to head for the hills...

So, we've been all over this great country visiting towns and camps everywhere we can. We mostly visit mining towns because plenty of folks in those kinds of towns need cheering up. Mining folks have hard lives, and a little fun is just what they need.

My mister says that folks are willing to work hard in a town like this because they have a chance at hitting a jackpot. A jackpot is when something super great unexpectedly comes to you. Jackpots are like picking out the right card at Monte. It doesn't happen to everyone. Just to a few of the lucky ones.

Folks come here with nothing and with one turn of the shovel, all that can change. Everyone is hoping for something better, and the best part is, that some actually find what they were hoping for, like me. I found my mister at the exact moment I needed him most. So, even though life can be hard sometimes, with a little hope, everyone, even a chicken, can hit the jackpot. If you don't believe it, just ask me.

Coloma, California 1848

My life at Sutter's Fort was much more stressful than life out here in the country. Sutter's Fort was such a busy place that us chickens had to watch our step in more ways than one. One time I got too close to the back end of a horse and that horse kicked me so hard that I popped out an egg! I went flying through the air, and the egg popped right out and hit the dirt where a bunch of other hens ran over and promptly started eating it.

Yes, we eat our own eggs, but it's not a good habit to get into. I knew of a hen who would lay an egg and promptly turn around and eat it. Her misses got so mad that she poked a hole in an egg, squeezed some hot pepper juice in it, then left it out for the hen to find. Let me tell you, that was the last time that hen ever ate an egg! But the hustle and bustle of my days at the fort are over. I'm a country hen now, and happy for it.

I remember the day we left Sutter's Fort. We were a small group of four wagons. We traveled most of the day and made camp on the banks of a river. Us chickens sleep in a crate right next to the tents at night, and during the day, we are free to scratch around and eat whatever we find. Mr. Marshall is in charge.

He is in search of his fortune, just like all those folks at Sutter's Fort were. There was always a steady stream of folks coming and going, all in search of their fortunes. I'm not sure what a fortune is, but it must be pretty important because a lot of those folks left their homes and families behind to find it. I think a fortune is probably a lot like a fat, juicy, potato bug. Potato bugs are hard to find because they live under the dirt, but if you scratch around rocks and under tree roots, you can sometimes find one. If you do, it's a tasty meal all by itself! I've only actually found a potato bug twice in my life, but I will never give up looking for them- they're that good. So, I guess the folks here are looking for their own version of potato bugs, whatever that might be.

Mr. Marshall is using the river to find his fortune. He says he's building a sawmill. I'm not sure why he needs the river to make his sawmill work, but he seems like a smart man, so I'm sure he can figure it out. I plan to do my part by providing him with an egg a day so he can have scrambled eggs and beans every morning.

There are ten of us hens living in camp, which is good because Mr. Marshall has hired lots of helpers to help him build his sawmill. They all get powerful hungry for eggs and beans. Most of the workers live in tents, but there are some who live in their own camp, called a village. Mr. Marshall calls them Indians, and they have lived by this river pretty much forever.

Some of the workers who came here with us from Sutter's Fort treat the Indians badly like they aren't very important because they're different on the outside. That reminds me of a hen I knew. She used to prance around and act like she was better than the rest of us because she laid pretty blue eggs. But I happen to know that the inside of her eggs looked and tasted just like a regular old brown egg, so what cause did she have to think she was something special?

One morning, I was chasing a grasshopper and I ended up in the Indian village. One of the misses tossed me a piece of acorn cake. It's like a pancake made of smashed-up acorns. I thought that was nice of her, I knew it must have taken a lot of work to get enough acorns to make that one cake. If I could have laid an egg for her to thank her, I would have, but I had already laid my egg for that day earlier in the morning. After I had my snack I headed down towards the water.

Now, though few things are better than a fatty potato bug, catching a small minnow in the shallow water is a very close second. I was always careful because that river sure was rushing fast and I didn't want it to carry me away. Today, the workers were busy digging near the water and making improvements to their sawmill. I wanted to get close enough to see if there were any potato bugs in the mounds of fresh dirt, but they kept shooing me away and I didn't want to get too close to their boots in case folks are like horses and might give me a swift kick.

So, I wandered down a ways in search of minnows. Looking down into the clear water I saw something golden colored and shiny. Now chickens love to peck at shiny things. When one of us hatches out some chicks, the missus always puts a couple of shiny buttons in the water dish so they will know where to find a drink. I always have to peck at shiny things. I can't help myself.

So, I pecked pretty hard at that gold sparkle rock, and to my surprise, I left a dent in it! That was unusual because most rocks I've known don't break when you peck them. That dented rock made me suspicious, so I decided to leave it alone. When I turned my head, sure enough, there was another golden, sparkle rock down the stream and another!

I was so distracted by the sparkly rocks that I didn't notice that Mr. Marshall was yelling at me to move out of the way. He headed toward me and was about to give me a not-so-gentle nudge when he glanced down at the water and saw what I was pecking at. He reached down and picked it up. He seemed surprised and excited at the same time.

He glanced around to make sure no one was watching, then he bent down and picked up the rest of those rocks, put them in his pockets, and walked back up the hill to camp. I thought those rocks must have been dangerous and he didn't want anyone else to know about them and get upset. They probably weren't even rocks at all. Everyone knows you can't put a dent in a rock!

Though I didn't know it at the time, those rocks turned out to be pretty important. So important that sometime later, work on the sawmill stopped completely. As it turned out, those rocks weren't dangerous. They were valuable and everyone wanted to get their hands on one. The workers all left their jobs at the sawmill and went out searching for golden sparkle rocks. Even the Indians got some shovels and started digging for gold rocks. I thought Mr. Marshall would be disappointed that he had no one left to work on his saw-mill, but he didn't seem disappointed, he went out looking for more of those rocks too!

I liked living in the country, but since we didn't have anyone who needed eggs for breakfast anymore, the misses had to pack up our camp, and we got back in the wagons and headed down the road away from the river. As we traveled, we passed by wagons and horses coming our way. There were folks everywhere all in a hurry to get down to the river and hunt up some sparkle rocks of their own. Soon, we passed by Sutter's Fort. I was shocked to see it deserted! Everyone had left to go out and look for their fortunes.

I heard later that Mr. Marshall was telling folks that he was the one to discover the rocks in the river. I didn't mind. Chickens don't care much for being famous. If it's not about food, we aren't overly concerned with it. You know, that nice Mr. Marshall never did manage to turn our discovery into a fortune for himself. He left the river and decided to start growing grapes.

That's a sight better idea than looking for yellow rocks. You can't eat rocks. The fact is, not many of those folks ended up finding their fortune there by that river. The way I heard it, so many people came looking for golden sparkle rocks that the ground ran out of them! I hope that never happens with potato bugs. But then, even if I never actually find another potato bug, it's the thought that I might find one that keeps me going. I think it's the same with fortunes. Looking for it is part of the fortune itself.

Fort Laramie, Wyoming Territory, 1846

I haven't always lived here at the fort. I was hatched in a faraway place called Missouri, and my folks took me and two other hens along for the ride on the Oregon Trail. Their idea was to take us with them and have fresh eggs for breakfast every day, but I think that by the time we got to Fort Laramie, and they realized that we weren't even halfway to Oregon yet, they decided that they had to leave us behind.

So, they traded the three of us for a sack of flour. I don't think that was a particularly good trade since everyone knows chickens are way better than a boring, old sack of flour, but at least now I can stay in one place, and I don't have to bump around in a wagon anymore.

My new missus is happy to have us because she runs a business here at the Fort and says she can use us in her business. Her business is a bakery and she's busy all the time. I try to lay as many eggs as I can so she can bake lots of buttermilk pies. Folks around here are crazy for her pies and they buy all the buttermilk pies she can bake. Every now and then a bit of it will show up in the supper scraps my missus tosses to us. I do love me some buttermilk pie.

Sometimes at night, I dream about my days on the Oregon Trail. You might think it was lonely out there, but you would be wrong about that. So many folks were rushing for Oregon that my mister used to say that you couldn't spit into the wind without hitting another wagon train heading west. Sometimes, there were so many wagons that we traveled three abreast, and let me tell you, the dust that churned up made it hard for us to breathe.

There were lots of dangers on the Oregon Trail. Folks were always worried about things, like Indian attacks, or getting snake bit, or falling out of the wagon while crossing the rivers. That one worried me too. Chickens can't swim, and falling out of the wagon in the middle of the river would have been the end of my trip on the Oregon Trail. But the one thing that worried folks the most was snow. It seemed like every time we stopped for the night folks would gather together and talk about snow. That didn't make any sense to me. I spent over 600 miles strapped in a crate to the back of a wagon and I didn't see a speck of snow anywhere, so why those wagon train folks were so worried about it all the time is a mystery to me.

Overall, I like my new life at Fort Laramie very much. There are always lots of trappers and Indians around who come in to do their trading and catch up on the gossip. Plus, with all the wagon trains coming through, there are always a lot of people milling about, writing letters, and making repairs to their wagons. I even got a chance to meet someone who became pretty famous, although I didn't know he was bound to be famous at the time.

His name was George, and he was pretty ordinary as far as folks go. He was leading a wagon train to Oregon and was very interested in a shortcut that some folks swore would get you to Oregon a month sooner than everyone else. This made me think of what my missus always says. She says that the only shortcut in life is hard work. I think she means that if you try to bake some bread quicker than the time it takes to do it right, it might look golden brown on the outside and smell good and tasty, but what you don't realize is that it's only done on the outside. The inside will be mushy, and no one wants to eat mushy bread. Except maybe chickens. Chickens will eat anything, and I do mean anything.

One afternoon, I happened to be scratching around in front of the bakery while George and another mister were leaning on the porch railing enjoying some of my missus' famous cinnamon rolls. I overheard George talking to Mr. Clyman about this Oregon Trail shortcut everyone was excited about. Mr. Clyman was what they called a "mountain man," which meant he had been around these parts for a long time and generally knew what he was talking about. He advised George not to take the shortcut, but George didn't seem to be too interested in what Mr. Clyman had to say. I think his mind was already made up.

He started to explain his thoughts on the issue, but I stopped listening because just then my missus came out with the supper scraps. She always called out in a high-pitched voice "Chickee-Chickee- Chickeeeeee," and let me tell you, every chicken in the fort comes running full speed at the sound of her voice. At supper scrap time, you never knew what you were going to get. You just knew it would be good.

She tossed a pail of scraps on the dirt, and we all swarmed it and grabbed as much as we could. While I was enjoying some tasty bits and pieces, I heard my new acquaintance George call out, "Is that chicken actually eating *chicken*?"

And my missus replied, "Yes sir, they eat any scraps I dump out. They aren't particular about it. We had fried chicken for our supper and now the chickens are having what's left!"

Mr. Clyman looked like he didn't much approve of that, but George just wrinkled his brow and had a thoughtful expression on his face.

Now I'm not saying that George got the idea from me, but I heard some time later that he and his whole wagon train got stuck in the snow on the way to Oregon, and let's just say they didn't starve to death, if you know what I mean. When word got down to us at the fort of what had happened in the mountains, people were pretty upset about it. I'm not sure why they were so upset. If you're hungry, you gotta eat, right?

Besides, my missus always says you can't understand a person until you have walked a mile in their shoes. Chickens don't wear shoes, so I'm not sure about the shoes part, but I think it means that until you've been in the same situation as someone else, you don't know what you would do. Still, folks seemed pretty high and mighty about their opinions on the subject and everyone insisted that they wouldn't have done it if it had been them.

One morning, the blacksmith's wife came over to visit with my missus and she brought a newspaper from California that told all about what happened to George Donner and his folks. I had to chuckle a bit. That reporter sat down with one of the survivors of the Donner Party and actually asked her what it tasted like, and you'll never believe what she said.

She said, "It tasted like chicken."

Cascade, Montana 1897

I get picked on a lot because I limp and kind of waddle when I walk. I've been this way ever since I hatched. It doesn't hurt too much, but I can't get anywhere fast, and that has made me timid. I know I can't outrun a fox or a bobcat, so I don't like to venture far from the coop. When all my fellow chickens are out scratching around, I do my scratching close to home.

When the missus throws us table scraps after dinner, I don't usually get there in time to get anything good. Even if I do get there in time, the other hens peck me and chase me away. Sometimes, after everyone has gotten what they wanted and run off with it, I scoot in, grab a potato peel, and run off with it so I can look like I got something good like everyone else. Then, I just leave that potato peel under a bush somewhere.

I'm sorry to say this, but chickens tend to pick on the weak ones. It's not one of our better qualities. I've let it become something that's normal to me, and I've even thought at times that it is what I deserve. But lately, I've been thinking that it's time I started sticking up for myself more. This is a lesson that I have been learning from my friend Missus Mary.

You may think that chickens and folks can't be friends, but we can. I learned this one evening when Missus Mary threw a whole bucket of dinner scraps for us chickens to scratch around in and see what we could find. We live in a place called a convent. It's a home run by missuses called sisters. It's for children who don't have anyone to care for them. With so many children around, there are a lot of table scraps, and sometimes there's some pretty tasty bits.

Of course, I don't know from experience, since there generally isn't anything left for me by the time I get there. Well, Missus Mary noticed that I was always getting pecked by the other hens and that I rarely got any of the scraps all the other hens were getting. One day, while everyone else was off enjoying their treats, I was scratching in the dirt seeing if there was anything left, and she took a tomato out of her apron pocket and tossed it in my direction. At first, I ran away as fast as I could because I thought she was throwing things at me to hurt me. See what I mean about meanness being normal to me? But she clicked her tongue at me softly and talked in such a nice voice that I came back around cautiously.

I pecked at that tomato and noticed it had a crack in it. I could just see inside, and I noticed it had a worm living in it. Now, a worm AND a tomato is like, double tasty, so I was excited about that. Plus, I was the only hen around, so I could stand right there in the yard and eat the whole thing all by myself.

That evening, as I settled down on the roost with a tummy full of worm and tomato, there was a cool breeze coming off the snowy mountains, and well, that was the best feeling I have ever had. That's how a small kindness when you need it most can make you feel.

After that, Missus Mary usually kept something in her pocket for me to have when all the rest of the hens had gotten everything else. That's why I was extra sad when she had to leave and go live in town. Even though she took care of all of us here at the convent, animals and folks alike, she had ways that the folks here didn't approve of. I don't know what that means. I just heard it said.

They call her Stagecoach Mary now because she uses a stagecoach to deliver the mail. That's her new job, she's been at it for a few years and apparently, it's a very important job. Usually, they only give that job to a mister, but Missus Mary is so strong and dependable she's only the second missus in the whole country to drive the mail around. When you drive the mail, you have to be all by yourself out in the wilderness where a bear or a mountain lion might try and eat you, but she isn't scared. That's why she was given the job. Folks like mail. I'm not sure why. It's just pieces of paper and you can't eat paper. But whenever someone here gets mail, they usually smile and sometimes even cry happy tears. I'm proud that our Missus Mary does such a special job.

I think the sisters miss having Mary around. Sometimes, I hear them talking, and once I heard them talk about how some folks in town are mean to Stagecoach Mary. Some folks don't like her because she used to be a slave. I think being a slave means you're always having to do what someone else tells you to do, and you can't ever do what you want. It's a very strange thing for me to think about because chickens get to do what we want. Folks don't tell us what to do.

I don't think the birds in the trees have to do what someone else says and neither do the squirrels and field mice. Being a slave must be something only folks make other folks be. I'm just a chicken, so I don't know lots of things like the folks do, but it doesn't sound like a very nice thing to do to someone.

Another reason folks are mean to Stagecoach Mary is because they say she looks different from the other folks around these parts. I don't see what they mean by that. She has arms and legs and a nose like everyone else. The only difference is she is a darker color, but it can't be that, can it? Us chickens are all different colors, but as long as we all have legs and beaks and feathers, that's all that matters, right?

Maybe folks are like chickens, and they try to push Stagecoach Mary around because they think she's weak because she's different. But the big difference between Stagecoach Mary and a chicken is that she doesn't let anyone push her around! I remember a time when a mister who worked here at the convent pushed Missus Mary to the ground and she grabbed her gun and shot at him! The sisters didn't like that much, but us chickens thought she did the right thing. Now, Missus Mary uses her gun to protect the mail. She's even gotten into fights with wolves when they try to steal the mail. Maybe the lesson we should learn from Missus Mary is that it's important to stick up for ourselves.

One thing I know for certain is that all the hard things that have happened to Stagecoach Mary haven't gotten her down. The sisters say that even though some folks are mean, she still has lots of friends in town. They say that most folks like Stagecoach Mary on account of her being nice to the children who live in town and also because she's always buying meals for folks who haven't been eatin' regular. I like that last part the best. Everyone knows how important meals are.

But maybe folks like her also because she's strong and doesn't let the mean folks make her feel bad. Maybe she's an example of how we should all be. Just because someone looks different or has different ways, that doesn't mean that they aren't as good as everyone else. I'm going to do my best to remember that and work hard at standing up for myself. Maybe if I stop running away every time a hen is mean to me, they'll learn that I'm not going to put up with their meanness anymore.

I want to be more like my friend Missus Mary, and not let others bring me down. Maybe next time Stagecoach Mary comes for a visit, she'll notice that I'm not running away anymore, and she will be proud of me. Maybe she will even bring me another tomato with a worm in it. I bet she will. That's the kind of thing friends always do for other friends, and I'm proud to call Stagecoach Mary my friend.

Wichita, Kansas 1875

⭐

I've lived here in Wichita all my life, which is about four years now. Four years is pretty old for a chicken, but since I'm a particular favorite of my missus, she takes good care of me and keeps me healthy. My missus runs a general store here in Wichita, and I'm valuable to her on account of how much I like to go broody. Going broody means something inside me tells me it's time to sit on eggs.

I don't really know why I do it, but I do, and magically, a few weeks later, I have a bunch of chicks to take care of. Most hens go broody once a year in the springtime, but I'm so fond of going broody that I do it three or four times a year in all seasons. My missus likes this because that means I will hatch dozens of chicks every year and she can sell them in the store. She lets me keep them and raise them until I am tired of them, and then they go to live with other folks, and that's fine with me.

I like to take my chicks out scratching around all over town and folks in town know me by now. They think my name is Broody, and that's what they call me. I guess folks are pretty dumb since they don't understand that broody isn't a name, it's a condition. But they always smile and point at me and say silly things like, "There goes

Broody with her latest flock of babies." Everyone knows that chickens have chicks, not babies. See what I mean about dumb?

I was out with my chicks one fine morning when the cattle herds were in. When the cattle herds are in town, there's always a lot of activity. The cowboys who drive the cattle through have been out on the prairie working, and they look forward to getting to town so they can have a good time. I like it better when it's quiet around here, but sometimes having a lot of folks in town makes things exciting.

On this particular day, it was double exciting because not only were the cowboys in town, but Professor Wollenford's Miracle Ointment show was in town too. From time to time, traveling medicine shows came here to Wichita. The shows only stayed a day or two, but folks sure liked to see the entertainment they put on. Sometimes, they had bands and singers, and sometimes people who could do tricks.

One time, the strongest man in the whole world actually came to Wichita with one of the shows! He could lift a grown man over his head like it was nothing! I guess all of this was entertaining for the folks, though. Us chickens aren't interested in such things. But, if the world's biggest grasshopper or longest worm ever come to town, I will sure take an interest!

On this particular day, there was a larger-than-normal crowd surrounding the show wagon. Most of the folks in the crowd were cowboys, and they were pretty loud and rowdy, even though it was only late morning. That professor had a man with him who was a juggler, and he could toss bottles around and catch them so quick that you could get dizzy just watching him. The cowboys sure thought he was something. I didn't think much of him, especially when he put his bottles down and started juggling eggs. Everyone sure thought that was special, but who cares if you can toss eggs around? Anyone can do that! I'd like to see him actually lay an egg. Now *that's* special! Since I was not impressed, I just ignored him and kept scratching around in front of the cigar store with my brood of nine chicks.

While we were enjoying some termites we found on the side of the boardwalk, Professor Wollenford had the cowboys roaring. He was telling them stories about all the things his miracle ointment could help them with. All I remember about the next few minutes was the Professor talking about how his ointment could cure saddle rash and for just one silver dollar the cowboys could find out for themselves. Well, those cowboys kept yelling out silly things and slapping each other on the back and having a good old time making fun of the Professor and his claims. So the Professor said he could prove it, he said his ointment was strong enough to take the feathers off of a chicken, and if it could do that, then it could surely take the rash off a cowboy's back side. I wasn't really paying much attention to all he said, I did perk up a bit at the word chicken, but I was distracted by two of my chicks fighting over a particularly big termite so I never saw what happened next coming.

The Professor sent that juggler over to me and before I even knew what was happening, he grabbed me, took a hold of my legs, flipped me so I was upside down, and carried me that way. He was even swinging me from one side to the next as he walked! Well, the cowboys thought this was the funniest thing they had ever seen. I couldn't see too well on account of being upside down, but all I could think about was my chicks. They were chirping and running in circles and not sure what to do. Luckily, I saw them scoot under the boardwalk, which made me relatively sure they wouldn't get stepped on.

I put up a fuss and flapped my wings as hard as I could. It was pretty humiliating to be upside down like that. I was also worried about how I would keep my chicks warm if the Professor's ointment took off all my feathers. Feathers are kind of important to us chickens. I heard a few folks in the crowd protest this treatment of me.

A man's voice shouted. "Hey, that's old Broody, she warn't hurtin' nobody!"

But mostly I heard the cowboys hootin' and yelling at the Professor to use his ointment and take my feathers off.

That juggler held me up in the air as high as he could and the Professor dug his fingers into his jar of miracle ointment. The world looked different from upside down, but I definitely noticed when the crowd parted to let a tall lawman through. He was a Deputy Marshall and everyone, except for Professor Wollenford and his juggler, knew that he wasn't one to put up with any shenanigans.

He talked low and firm to that juggler. I was too distracted to hear what he said, but I sure took notice when that lawman took out his gun and clunked that no-talent juggler on the back of his head! He fell straight to the ground dropping me as he went. I flapped my wings hard and got myself mostly upright. I somersaulted once through the force of hitting the dirt, but I was still spry enough to pop up and take off running. I ran straight to my chicks and all ten of us took off, tearing down an alley. I don't know what was said that made Deputy Marshall clunk that man. Maybe that lawman just explained to him that getting laughs at someone else's expense was never a good thing to do.

I heard later that afternoon that the lawman made Professor Wollenford and his juggler pack up and leave town right then and there. They didn't even get a chance to sell any of their saddle rash ointment to the cowboys. I think most people were fine with seeing them go since I'm kind of important around Wichita and folks didn't like seeing me treated badly. Plus, seeing the lawman clunk that juggler was plenty more exciting than watching the juggler toss bottles in the air.

I never did see that Deputy Marshall again so I could thank him. At the next election, he got voted out, and I heard that he became a lawman in some place called Tombstone. I wonder if he'll run into old Professor Wollenford there? I bet if he does that juggler will remember the headache he got in Wichita, and he won't be so quick to grab citizens who are just minding their own business off the street and swing them around upside down! As for me, I'll always be grateful when I remember the time Deputy Marshal Wyatt Earp saved my feathers.

Buckland Station, Nevada 1861

I ended up in Buckland Station after the folks who hauled me all the way from the east on their covered wagon took one look at the mountains ahead and decided to leave us chickens behind. I'm not sorry about that. I was pretty tired of riding in a crate tied to the back of the wagon. It was very dusty, and we hardly ever got to get out of the crate and run around. I was excited to go west, but I guess I'm just about as far west as I will ever get, and that's fine with me.

Because Buckland Station is a trading post, it's quite a lively place. There are always people coming and going. The wagon trains stop here on their way to Oregon and California. You have to go over the mountains to get to those places, so folks are happy to stop and rest a while and get their courage up before they face the long trail ahead. I'm not sure what's so great about Oregon and California that folks would risk their lives to get there. Us chickens aren't much for traveling. As long as we have a place to sleep, a handful of grain to eat, and maybe a grubworm or two, we're content.

The only problem with this place is that sometimes the other chickens who live here pick on me because I'm small. I'm a type of chicken called a bantam. Bantams are exactly like other chickens except we're smaller. Sometimes I take a lot of grief for being smaller than the others. I used to get pretty down about it at times, but that was before Buckland Station became a stop on the Pony Express route.

The Pony Express is a way for folks to send messages to other folks who live far away. I'm not sure why folks are so interested in what's going on in other places when there's so much going on right here to be interested in. But they are, and the Pony Express is important to them.

I mentioned that the Pony Express helped me be less down about being small. Do you know why? Because folks who want to ride the horses for the Pony Express have to be small too! That's how they get the messages from one place to another. Small misters ride on a horse until the horse is too tired to go fast, and then, they hop on another horse, and off they go! It's important to be small. If you're a biggun, they won't let you ride for them because it will make the horse too tired. So you see, being little has its advantages!

One rider in particular made an impression on me. His name was Robert Haslam, but everyone called him "Pony Bob." He became famous for being the one to ride the farthest in the shortest amount of time. Doing things quickly is important to folks, but not so important for chickens. Well, one time they had Pony Bob riding all over the place, and it got a bit dangerous because of the Indians.

Indians are folks who live out on the prairie, and they're angry because other folks came and started living on their land without asking first. I don't blame the Indians for being mad about that. Us chickens follow a pecking order, and new chickens to the flock definitely shouldn't be trying to take the best places on the roost.

Anyways, Pony Bob had been riding and riding for more time than I can even think about, and when he got to Buckland's he was supposed to hand his messages over to another mister who was supposed to get on a horse and continue on. But that mister refused to go because he was scared of the Indians. I know all this because I was scratching around by the porch where the misters were talking about it. I was so interested in what they were saying that I didn't notice that a mangy dog that had come west with a passing wagon train was sneaking up on me.

Sometimes dogs think they can try to catch me and eat me because I'm small and not as big and scary as other roosters. Well, I turned just in time. When that dog lunged at me I ruffled my feathers, jumped up, and used my super sharp spurs to cut him right below his ear. He yelped with more surprise than pain. I don't think he was expecting a little thing like me to put up much of a fight, but he wasn't through yet. He circled me and got a hold of my tail feathers. If you think that didn't hurt, you're crazy! It was hard for me to fight back with my rear nearly completely in his mouth, but I managed to twist around and peck his nose as hard as I could.

He let go, and I jumped up again and cut him on the shoulder. Then, again, a second later, and got him just under the eye. I guess that did it because he started whining and slunked away with his tail between his legs. Even though I had lost quite a bit of my tail feathers and I was feeling pretty sore, I threw my head back and let out the loudest crow I could, partly for victory and partly to tell that dog I was ready any time he wanted to come back for more!

After all that, I turned around and saw I had an audience. Mr. Buckland and Pony Bob were standing on the porch watching me, and right then and there Pony Bob decided to finish that Pony Express route on his own even though he was tired and the Indians might get him. I'm not saying that my fight with the dog inspired him to go, but maybe seeing a little guy like me face up to a big, mean dog reminded him that we might be little, but we can sure accomplish great things when we need to.

As it turned out, he finished that route without even seeing an Indian and I heard from some folks talking outside of a tent that the message that he carried was a very special one. It was a message that let all the folks in these parts know that we had a new President. A President is like a rooster, but instead of being in charge of all the chickens in the coop, he's in charge of all the folks in the country. The new president was named Abraham Lincoln. Having a new rooster in the coop is a pretty big deal so I bet folks appreciated Pony Bob getting them the news in record time.

I know I'm not the one who made that long ride, but I like to think that my battle with that dog showed Pony Bob that he could do great things. It's nice to know that we may never do anything great ourselves, but we can be the ones to inspire someone else to, and in a way, that's just as important.

Promontory Summit, Utah Territory, 1869

A train looks like a giant caterpillar, except you can't eat it. That's a shame because a juicy caterpillar makes a very satisfying lunch. I know a lot about lunch and also a lot about trains because Mr. Lee and I are busy building something called the transcontinental railroad. Well, we aren't exactly the ones building it. Mr. Lee cooks the food, and I provide the eggs he uses to cook with, so we do have a very important part since the folks doing the building need good meals to keep up their strength.

Mr. Lee named me "Ji," which is how you say "chicken" in his language. I know that's not the most creative name, but since most chickens go their whole lives without ever having a name, I'm not complaining. A name is what makes you special. Mr. Lee is Chinese. I'm not Chinese. I was hatched here in America, but since I spend all my time in the Chinese camp and know all the Chinese ways, Mr. Lee says I'm what they call "American-born Chinese." That makes me proud because the Chinese are hard workers. No one works harder at building the railroad than they do.

Mr. Lee used to be a builder. In fact, that's how we met. It was a few years back when they were blasting a hole through the mountain for the train to go through. Who came up with that dumb plan, I'll never know. Mr. Lee was very brave. They would lower him down the mountain, and he would hang in a basket tied with ropes. Then, he would drill a hole in the rock, put a red stick in the hole, and light it on fire. Well, that red stick was magic because it made a huge sound and a lot of smoke, and when it was over, there would be a hole in the rock that would help make a tunnel through the mountain.

One time, something went wrong and the stick caused what they called a rock avalanche. That's how Mr. Lee got his leg smashed. The camp doctor did the best he could to put his leg back together, but now Mr. Lee has to walk with a cane, and he's in a lot of pain sometimes. But Mr. Lee refuses to complain because three men died in that rock avalanche. Having to walk with a limp just reminds him how lucky he is.

I don't remember meeting Mr. Lee. Chickens don't have great memories, and I was still a pullet at the time, barely four months old. Sometimes in the late afternoon, we take a break and I jump up on Mr. Lee's lap, and he pets my feathers around my neck and tells me the story of how we first met. When he first saw me, I had a hurt leg too. He says I was chasing a beetle and was limping as fast as I could. But just as I was about to snatch that beetle, another chicken beat me to it and got it ahead of me.

He said I never stopped trying though, and that was a sign to him that he should not stop trying even though he had a bad leg now too. Mr. Lee says I am a double sign to him because he was born in the year of the rooster, and even though I'm not a rooster, he says I'm close enough. I'm not quite sure what being a sign means. I just know that it means that I will never be chopped up and stir-fried, so I guess being a sign is a great thing.

Mr. Lee can't hang in the baskets anymore on account of his bad leg. Since he didn't want to have to go back to China, he convinced the camp boss that he could cook as good as his old popo back in China. The boss mister gave him a try. Now, Mr. Lee spends his days cooking and making sure the men who eat with us are healthy and strong. I lay as many eggs as I can so Mr. Lee can use them in the soup and custard and rice.

Mr. Lee knows that if the men get to eat food cooked in the Chinese way, it will make their hearts and their bellies happy. Sometimes, some of the Irish railroad workers will walk by our tent and smell the food Mr. Lee's cooking, and I can tell by the looks on their faces that they wished they could eat in the Chinese way. All the Irish eat are potatoes and everyone knows there's no flavor in potatoes.

My favorite time of the day is the evening meal when all the men come in for their supper. They're always very tired, and sometimes they're angry on account of the fact that the Chinese get paid less than the Irish for doing the same work. That doesn't seem fair to me, and I know Mr. Lee feels the same way, but he tries to make them feel better about it by feeding them a good meal.

He also makes sure they have plenty of tea to drink so their minds will feel better. The best part is after dinner when Mr. Lee tells stories of the old days in China. Sometimes the men laugh so hard you can hear it all over the camp, and sometimes the stories make them have tears in their eyes, tears from remembering. Chickens don't have stories, but I wish we did.

Today, Mr. Lee and I have the evening off because the railroad has provided a special meal for all the Chinese to celebrate that today the tracks finally connected and all of America can go from one side to the other on the train. I don't usually go down to where all the workers are because I don't want one of the Irish to see me and wonder if I might taste better than potatoes, but I did sneak down there today to watch the ceremony.

Some important men came in on a silver train. They were all dressed in a lot of clothes, even though the day was warm. They had on funny tall, flat-topped hats. Not practical, cone-shaped hats, like the Chinese wear. I knew their heads must be sweaty in those hats since the sun didn't slide down the sides like it does in Chinese hats. Maybe all that sunshine had an effect on them because they sure had a lot of trouble when they tried to hammer in the spikes.

A Chinese man can hammer a spike in two or three blows, but these fancy men couldn't even aim well enough to hit the spike! On top of that, they used funny gold-colored spikes that weren't spikes at all. As soon as they were done, they took them back out, put them in their pockets, and left!

Then a Chinese crew came in and hammered in the final real spikes. I guess those fancy men will tell everyone that they hammered in the last spikes when really it was the Chinese who did it. After all that, everyone posed for a photograph. Lots of folks were upset when they heard about the photograph since almost all the Chinese were at the special meal and weren't asked to be in the photo at all.

Mr. Lee says that we shouldn't worry and that someday there will be a celebration for the Chinese railroad builders and all of

America will be grateful for the work we did here. I don't know if that will ever happen. Mr. Lee gets some crazy ideas sometimes, like the time he said that someday folks all over America will pay money to go and eat at restaurants that only sell Chinese food. Ha! Who thinks that will ever happen?

Many weeks later, I was just settling down for the night, and I got to have a good look at that picture of the ceremony. Mr. Lee always sets a newspaper under my roost in our tent in case I have to relieve myself in the night, so when I hopped up on the roost and looked down, there was that picture on the front page of the newspaper. If you look closely at that picture, on the left-hand side there is a small dot, just to the side of a group of misters in the picture. That small dot is part of my foot. The rest of me is hidden behind them. Although I didn't set out to be in that picture, I'm glad that I am because I'm proud to represent the Chinese and all we did to bring America together.

My name is Ji, and I helped build the transcontinental railroad, one egg at a time.

Fort Smith, Arkansas, 1889

O ur mister is named Judge Parker, and folks call him a "hanging judge." I'm not sure what a "hanging judge" is, but one
time, a hen I know was jumping up the ladder to get to the highest
part of the roost, and somehow she got her toe caught in a gap in
the wood. When she jumped, she got jerked back, lost her balance,
and flipped upside down. No matter how hard she flapped she just
couldn't right herself.

Since she was just hanging there, she did the only thing she
could do. She put up a fuss. Once she started fussing, three or four
of the rest of us started cackling too, and let me tell you, we made a
racket they could probably hear all the way down at the fort. Well,
all that noise brought our missus out to see what was the matter,
and she quickly helped that hen get right side up again. So, I guess a
"hanging judge" is someone who hangs people upside down by their
toes until they say they won't do bad things anymore.

Speaking of folks who do bad things. There is sure no shortage
of them out here in these parts. There are so many bad people out
and about that the Judge had to hire a whole flock of deputies to go
out and find them. A lot of the bad folks are wandering around out

on the prairie lost, so they can't find the jail themselves. That's what the deputies are for. They find the bad folks and help them get to the jail.

Though there are lots of deputies, my favorite is Deputy Bass Reeves. One time, he was riding his horse down our street, and when he saw us pecking around in the yard, he reached in his saddle bag and pulled out his lunch sack. Then, he tossed us a nice, big piece of cornbread. Whoever came up with the idea to make bread out of corn is my personal hero because there's nothing tastier than cornbread. When Deputy Reeves shared his with us, well, that's a kindness I won't soon forget.

Deputy Reeves is pretty popular with the Judge and with other folks around town because he's especially good at finding lost bad folks. One time, I saw him riding down the street with no less than thirteen of them chained one to another following behind his horse! The Judge was going to need a real long roost to hang all those folks by their toes!

But not everyone in town is fond of Deputy Reeves. Can you believe that there are some who think he shouldn't be allowed to chain white bad folks up because Deputy Reeves himself has dark skin? Really? Now I know chickens have brains the size of a raspberry (speaking of raspberries- yum!), but even I know there is no logic in that. If light-skinned folks don't want Deputy Reeves to come huntin' for them, they should just not do bad things. Then they won't have to worry about it! Problem solved. Case closed. Ha! Maybe I should be a judge! No. Chickens can't be judges. We're too short.

Another famous person around Fort Smith is a missus named Belle Starr. She's famous for being bad, but she isn't lost, she lives right outside of town and even comes into Judge Parker's court to talk about her badness sometimes. I don't know if the Judge has ever hung her upside down by her toes, but he did send her out of town to a faraway jail so she could think about all the bad things she's done. I'm not sure how all that thinkin' was supposed to help. Us chickens aren't very big thinkers, but I don't think it worked in Missus Belle's case because she's home now, and she hasn't stopped doing bad things.

One thing that causes trouble for Missus Belle is she likes to get married all the time. She keeps marrying these misters who get her into all sorts of trouble. One of those misters showed her how to steal horses and now she does that all the time! I don't know why she does that. You can only ride one horse at a time, so why does she need more than one?

I think she needs some time away from all those misters. Look at us chickens. We don't get married, and I have never heard of a chicken who stole a horse. Another reason she shouldn't get married all the time is because every mister she marries ends up dead! Now I know I'm no expert when it comes to marriage since it isn't something I have ever done, but if I was a mister, I sure wouldn't marry Missus Belle on account of what's happened to her other misters! But she always manages to find someone who doesn't mind taking the risk. Although the one she has now doesn't seem to like her very much.

I once overheard someone ask the Judge why he does the job he does; punishing bad folks. The Judge said that bad folks are like snakes in a chicken coop. If you have a chicken coop, there are always going to be snakes. There's no stopping that. Snakes come in to help themselves to a couple of eggs for breakfast. Most snakes just do it because they're hungry, and stealing eggs is easier than working for them.

But every now and then you run into a snake that's a little more than just hungry. He told that man about the snake that came into our coop one night looking for some eggs, and when he didn't find any he grabbed a chicken off the roost, strangled her, and then tried to eat her. He was able to swallow her head and neck, but then had to spit her back out because he couldn't fit the rest of her in his mouth. What kind of snake thinks he can swallow a full-grown chicken whole like that? That was a pretty sad day for us chickens because we had never seen a snake act like that. What made it worse was the next night he came back and did the same exact thing again! Either he was the dumbest snake in the whole world to think it would somehow turn out different when it didn't work the day before, or he did it straight out of meanness. I don't know which.

When the Judge found that second dead hen with her head and neck slimed too, he sent his son out with a shotgun to wait for that snake. Let's just say that snake won't be killing any more chickens. I think that's how it is with bad folks. Some of them haven't ever learned the right way to behave, and the Judge tries his best to teach them. Some of them are just downright mean, like that snake was, and there is no teaching them anything. They have to be stopped before they hurt more folks.

I guess you could say I'm proud to live with Judge Parker, and what he does helps keep us all safe. I'm also proud to call Deputy Reeves my friend. In fact, I'm pretty sure we're best friends. Everyone knows that you don't share your cornbread with just anybody.

South Pass City, Wyoming Territory, 1870

The problem with roosters is that they think they are much more important than they really are. The rooster who lives with us is a bothersome bird. He often struts around and clucks to trick us into coming over because we think he's found something good to eat that he wants to share with us. When we get there, we find out he hasn't found anything at all. He's just trying to get our attention. Honestly, who's got time for that? Another problem with roosters is that they're always fighting over nothing. They are very sensitive and get their hackles up, then they think they have to holler and fight to make sure everyone notices them. Such a waste of energy.

I live in South Pass City in the territory of Wyoming. My missus is named Missus Esther Hobart, and she is very well known in these parts. You see, she had an idea that womenfolk should get to do the things that the menfolk got to do. She started talking about it around here, and believe it or not, folks listened. Our town is the first town in the world to give all the womenfolk the right to vote.

Voting is when folks help decide how to make things fair for everyone. That's pretty important. I wonder why women folk didn't get to decide on that before? It must be different in the folks' world because in the chicken world hens are every bit as capable as roosters for most things. Once I saw a mama hen fight off a hawk that was threatening to carry away one of her babies. Another time I saw a hen peck the living daylights out of a snake that was trying to steal her eggs. Where was the rooster when all of that was going on? Out under a shade tree preening and making sure his feathers were all nice and shiny!

Now, you might think I am saying all menfolk are like preening roosters, but that couldn't be farther from the truth. In fact, it was that nice neighbor of ours, Mr. Bright, who helped our missus with the whole idea that womenfolk should vote. He got the other menfolk to agree with him and that's when our territory became the first place to let all the missuses vote.

Not all the menfolk were happy about this. Some thought women should just stay home and tend to the children and make the dinners. One of the important misters got really upset about it. He said he would quit his job unless everyone changed their minds and forgot the whole idea of women voting. Well, no one changed their mind and that mister ended up quitting. That's when other folks decided that our missus should take his job and she became the first missus to become a Justice of the Peace!

A Justice of the Peace is a really important thing to be. I know a lot about it because I like to watch through the windows and see what's going on in our house when my missus is Justice of the Peace-ing. How it works is folks come and stand in a line in front of her, then, they all argue about someone who has done them wrong. Our missus decides who argues the best and what should be done about the problem.

I'm not sure why folks need so much help deciding an argument. Us chickens just do what comes into our heads to do, and it mostly turns out right. For example, one time I was sitting on a whole passel of eggs and another hen jumped up and squished in with me in the nesting box. I knew she was up to no good, and I sure was right! That night, when I was just dozing off, she tried to slide some of my eggs under her feathers. Well, I sure didn't need a Justice of the Peace to decide things for me. I just took those eggs back and gave her a couple of strong pecks to her head, and the problem was solved. Maybe the folks should watch us chickens and handle things more the way we do.

There's more to being a Justice of the Peace than just listening to folks argue. Occasionally, when our missus doesn't like what they have to say, she locks them up in jail. Jail is kind of like being stuck in the hen house on a lovely spring day when there are lots of grasshoppers outside, and all you can do is look at them and imagine how tasty they must be.

Everyone in our town is proud of my missus. They know she must be powerful smart to have a job like that. Remember what I was saying about roosters? Well, one day our mister was fussing and yelling and making a ruckus at the missus. He does that mostly when he drinks too much water from a bottle. He gets this water at special houses in town that are called saloons. Some of the men folks in these parts are fond of drinking their water like that, but that water must be sour because all it does is make them loud and angry.

Folks should just drink water out of a puddle or a regular old water pail like we do. Well, our mister finished off a whole bottle of that rotten water, and he could sure be a mean old rip when he was drinking too much bottled water like he was that day. The missus just sent him to jail where all he could do was watch the grasshoppers out of the jailhouse window. Now, that's the way to deal with a rooster needing attention!

Some folks thought letting the womenfolk vote was all a big joke. Some others saw it as a way to get more womenfolk to come and live in our territory. I guess I don't care why they did it. I'm just glad they did. Overall, most folks saw our missus as a hero because she was showing the world that womenfolk are just as smart and capable as menfolk. What I don't understand is, why doesn't the world know that already?

Duncans Mills, California 1880

M y mister and missus run the general store here in Duncans
Mills. It's my job to make sure I lay plenty of eggs to supply
the store because our town has become quite a busy place. At first,
the only folks I would see around town were misters who worked at
cutting trees down. They would send them to places without trees
so other folks could have some trees to give them shade. Nowadays
people come here all the time for something they call a vacation. I'm
not sure what a vacation is. Chickens never go on vacation, but folks
seem to like these vacations, and they like to eat eggs when they are
on vacation, so I have my work cut out for me.

My life is overall pleasant, for the most part, because I'm popular. Popular means you're someone other folks like to talk about
when you're not around. I'm not sure why folks like to talk about
me. The only reason I can figure is because I have feathers on my
legs. That's the only difference between me and the other chickens
in town. I guess folks aren't used to seeing a chicken who looks like
me because they're always pointing at me and trying to pet me. Most
of us chickens don't like to be petted. It just isn't something that
comes natural to us, but I tolerate it because I guess when you're

popular, you have to put up with some things that other folks don't have to put up with.

You're probably wondering how a chicken like me ended up here in this small town. Well that's quite a story to tell. I'm one of the few chickens to ever ride on a stagecoach. You might think that riding on a stagecoach is a pretty fun thing to do, but truthfully, it wasn't fun at all. It was a very long, dusty, hot, crowded ride. You see, my missus ordered me special because she wanted to have a chicken that folks would be interested in looking at because then they would stop and buy something from her store. So, I left the farm where I was hatched, got packed up into a crate that was strapped to the top of a stagecoach, and off I went.

One of the most troublesome problems with riding on a stage-coach is that you're shoved in with lots of other folks you don't know and maybe don't want to spend the day with. That's what happened to me. I wasn't alone in my crate. There were two others in there with me. I wouldn't have cared so much if they were other chickens, but they weren't. They were guinea hens, and believe me when I tell you, no one likes guinea hens. I think my missus ordered them be-cause she made a mistake and thought they would be popular too, but it didn't take long for everyone in our town to start hating those guinea hens.

The biggest problem with guinea hens is that they're loud. They're always squawking about one thing or another. Another big problem with them is that they wander around everywhere and don't ever stay home. They like to roost in the trees and the missus can never get them to come down and stop bothering folks. But the absolute worst problem with guineas is that they are ugly. I mean

REALLY ugly. But the strange thing is they weren't always ugly. We were all hatched together, and I remember when I was little I used to be jealous of the little guineas because there is nothing cuter than a baby guinea.

When they first hatched they had such pretty markings on their faces, and even me with my feathers on my legs couldn't get all the attention. Everyone was always wanting to gush over the guineas. But the strangest thing happened as we grew older. Those guineas got uglier and uglier! Soon they lost all the feathers on their heads and their heads started looking like pointy pine cones! And there I was, stuck on top of a stagecoach with them for thirteen hours straight.

It was boring for most of the trip until something quite out of the ordinary happened. We were going down the road, minding our own business when all of a sudden, a man with a flour sack over his head stepped out and hollered at us! He had a gun, which made all the folks on the stagecoach nervous. I figured he just wanted a ride but he never got on, so that wasn't it. Then, I got worried that he was after me due to the fact that I'm popular, but that wasn't it either. He pointed his gun around and one lady offered him her purse but he very politely refused. Instead, he made the driver throw down a box with some papers and sacks in it. He took those, and off he went! It seemed to me to be quite a waste of time for all of us, himself included, but the folks on the stagecoach were definitely worked up about it.

I heard later that the man called himself Black Bart. He named himself after a pirate who lived long ago. A pirate is a mister who lives on a boat, which is something that scoots across the water like a duck. I'm not sure why Black Bart thinks he's a pirate. So far, I haven't seen much water around these parts. From what I could understand from the conversations I overheard at the general store, folks like him because he's always very polite when he's robbing folks, and even leaves poems behind for the folks to read. A poem is a message that says things in ways that are hard to understand, so most folks just end up pretending to know what poems mean.

My stagecoach ride was several years ago, but from what I hear, Black Bart is still at it. Every so often all the folks in town will start talking about him again and how he's still stopping stagecoaches and still leaving poems. One afternoon, after the news of his latest robbery came into town, it made me start thinking. If popular means that folks talk about you when you aren't around, then maybe he's popular too. I didn't much care for that notion because by the way folks talked about him, I could tell they didn't like him much. Maybe being popular isn't such a great thing to be after all?

While I was scratching around and thinking about all this I was interrupted by those blasted guineas up in a redwood tree making a ruckus for no reason at all. I began to realize that those guineas might be ugly and have strange ways, but they had never been mean or rude to me at all. Their ugliness was all on the outside, not the inside where it counts.

I decided right then and there that I was wrong for looking down my beak at those guineas. Maybe thinking mean about them was ugly, and I sure didn't want to be popular for being bad, like Black Bart. Besides, if I had to start wearing a flour sack on my head it's sure for certain that I wouldn't be able to catch any tasty bugs to eat. Maybe being popular isn't all that it's cracked up to be. At least that's what I think.

Gonzalez, Texas 1835

I t's not many who can say they had a part in history, but I had a part in the Texas Revolution, and here is my story...

Chickens are, by nature, very curious creatures, so naturally I was itching to get a good look at the thing the folks called a cannon that they had hid in the barn. To me, it looked like a huge, brown corn cob. I didn't know for sure that it was a corn cob. It was shaped like one, and trust me, there is nothing better than a good, half-eaten corn cob. Sometimes, after dinner, when the missus throws the scraps out to us chickens, I will get a hold of a corn cob, drag it under a mesquite bush, and spend a very happy hour picking it clean.

So, when all the visiting folks had arrived, they pulled that cannon out of the barn and everyone had a good time walking around it and having a look. I waited until they finally headed in for supper. Then, I went over to it and with one peck discovered it was definitely not corn, so I headed under the porch to hunt scorpions and listen in on the house conversations.

The folks said that cannon would come in handy when their revolution finally got going. Now, I had no idea what a revolution was, or how the cannon was going to help them with it. The closest I could come to understanding was that a revolution was an attempt to disrupt the pecking order. I know all about the pecking order. That's when the biggest, strongest chickens get to eat first and sleep at the top of the roost. Every now and then a young chicken, usually a rooster, will challenge that order. I've seen my share of rooster fights, and regardless of who wins or loses, both end up bloody at the end, so revolutions are not for me.

With my beak full of mashed scorpion, I heard the thump, thump, thump of a man walking down the porch steps, likely to get some quiet time because it sure was noisy in there. The folks were fussing and all talking at once. They sure were excited about that cannon. I swallowed hastily and headed out to see if the man had anything good to eat that he was willing to share. He was a familiar face. He had been to our house several times before and folks called him Davy Crocket.

But still, I kept my distance from him at first because a good rule of thumb is to stay out of catching distance in case the folks in the house were still hungry and sent this man out to do something about it. But when he tossed me a piece of his tortilla I couldn't help but come closer because, hey, who doesn't like a tasty piece of warm tortilla? I was almost within snatching distance of the tortilla when I looked up and froze in terror. Davy Crocket had a giant raccoon sleeping on top of his head!

Now raccoons are the mortal enemies of all chickens everywhere. There are certainly plenty of predators in search of chicken dinners that we have to be on the lookout for, but raccoons are the meanest. One time, the missus was planning on taking a hen to market in the morning and left her in a wooden crate on a bench on the porch the night before. A raccoon came over in the night, went underneath the bench, pulled the chicken's toes through the slats of the crate one at a time, and bit them off! All of them!

I don't think chicken toes are super tasty, so it just seemed to me that he did it out of meanness. Well, when the missus woke up and saw what had happened, she was very upset. The mister was all for taking that poor hen straight to the chopping block, but the missus said she had suffered enough and put her in a box in the barn until she was well enough to rejoin the flock. She named her "Stumpy", since those toes never did grow back. That chicken learned to do her scratchin' with her nubs, and the missus treated her like a pet. She brought her little treats almost every day and buried her under an oak tree when she died many years later. This just goes to show you that sometimes the worst day of your life can turn into the best day of your life, you just don't know it at the time.

Anyways, back to Mr. Crocket. On closer inspection, I was relieved to see that it wasn't a sleeping raccoon. It was a raccoon skin. That's when I realized that this man was a raccoon killer, and that made him at the top of the pecking order as far as I was concerned. Sometime later, I found out that he got killed at a place called the Alamo, and I was genuinely sad to hear it. Any man who will share his tortilla with you is a good man.

So back to my story, I promised to tell you how I had a part in the Texas Revolution, and here it is. A couple of days before Mr. Crockett shared his lunch with me, I had been out in the tall grass chasing down a moth. Moths aren't good eating, but it was something to do, and I don't like to be bored. Since it was a sunny day, the missus and her daughter were out doing the laundry. They had some dresses and shirts lying on top of the grass, drying in the sun. I chased that moth right up to that drying laundry. I knew better than to walk on top of it, so when the moth flew over, I gave up the chase and turned around to head back. That's when it happened. I didn't mean for it to happen. It just isn't something I ever think about. When you gotta go, you gotta go. I pooped right on top of the pretty white dress that was drying there in the sun. The missus must have turned in my direction just in time because she let out a howl that sent me jumping and sprinting to join the rest of the flock in the front yard.

While I was running, I could hear the daughter join in the fuss. She was crying and kept yelling about how her wedding dress was ruined. I don't know what a wedding dress is, but it must have been important because they gathered it up and rushed down to the river to wash it all over again. Unfortunately, myself and some of my colleagues had enjoyed a few branches of low hanging dewberries that morning and dewberries tend to cause a bit of a stain, so the missus was not successful in getting the spot off that dress. Lucky for me I am just a plain old red hen with no distinguishing marks so I just blend in with all the other hens. The missus never knew who was to blame for the whole event.

I felt pretty bad about it because it truly had been a careless mistake, but imagine my surprise today when everyone gathered at the cannon again, and I saw the missus and her daughter unroll a large piece of white material between two sticks. They had cut up that wedding dress into a big square and on it, they had painted a picture of the cannon. They had also painted a large black star right over the stain made by my dewberry poop!

Underneath it, they wrote the words "Come and Take It," which got the whole crowd fired up when they read it. My guess is that they weren't going to let anyone take that cannon from them. I can relate because when I'm hunkered down with a tasty corn cob, if anyone thinks they're going to get that away from me, they can just come and try and take it! That whole crowd of people marched that cannon under the flag and through the one street town of Gonzalez. I don't know what became of that flag or what happened in their revolution, but I'm proud that my poop had a part in it. I guess it's true that good can come from even some of your worst mistakes.

Unassigned Lands, Guthrie, Oklahoma Territory, 1889

My mister and missus are immigrants. Immigrants are folks who come from far away to live in a new place. I'm an immigrant too because I was hatched in St. Louis, and now I live way out on the prairie. Immigrants come to America for a better future. I'm not sure what that means because chickens don't ever think about the future. We are more of a "live in the moment" type of creature. Even though life is hard out here, my mister and missus go to sleep happy every night because they have their very own homestead.

I first started living with them back when we were in St. Louis. They came from a place called Germany and came to live with my mister's brother and his family who had a store that sold vegetables to folks. I was happy to live with them because there were always plenty of rotten vegetables that us chickens got to eat. Folks don't like rotten vegetables, but chickens love them. The mushier the better. Too bad the brother didn't have a worm store or a caterpillar store. I bet rotten worms and caterpillars are good eatin'. Or maybe even a roly-poly store. Roly-polies have a nice crunch to them, but I bet a squishy one would be even better.

Life in our small coop behind the vegetable store was pretty great, but my mister and missus were having a hard time being shoved in with the brother's family and all those vegetables. That's why they decided to head out to get their own homestead. I wasn't sure if moving to the prairie was a good idea. Of course, no one asked me. They just packed us all up and strapped us to the back of a covered wagon and off we went. My mister's brother suggested that us chickens stay in St. Louis, but my mister said we were a part of his plan, and we had to go with them. Why are folks always making so many plans? Chickens don't plan anything and we do alright.

Well, I thought we were just going to ride up to our new homestead and get scratching, but as it turned out, we didn't actually *have* a homestead at that point. It seems if we wanted a place to live we were going to have to race for it. Us chickens know all about racing. If one of us gets a hold of something tasty, then the race is on. The rest of us will chase after her and try to get it out of her mouth, and we don't stop for anything.

That's about what happened on that spring day when my mister went out racing for our land. We had arrived several days before and unhitched the wagon at the Deer Creek Train Station where the race was set to start. There were hundreds of people there who had the same idea as we had. I suspected my mister was a fast runner, but I wasn't sure if he could beat all those people. Of course, I didn't know about the plan then, or the rules.

Folks seem to be really interested in rules. It seems like they're always making up new rules for everything. This race had a bunch of rules, and one of them was that you couldn't start early. That way, no one would be able to get to where they were going sooner than anyone else. My mister thought that was a fair rule, but he said there weren't any rules about just having a look around ahead of time, so that's what he did.

He went out there at night, when the moon was full, and looked for a good place to race to. He had to hide himself and his horse in the bushes sometimes because if he got caught sneaking around out there, they wouldn't let him race, and then, we would have to go back to the vegetable store. I was secretly hoping he would get caught because I sure didn't see any folks selling vegetables at the train station, and a nice mushy carrot would have been good right about then.

Finally, the day of the race came, and if you can believe it, there were even more people there ready to race than when we first arrived. Back in the day when I lived in a proper chicken coop, us hens used to pile into one nesting box to lay our eggs even though there were three boxes to choose from. We would smash in four or five of us in one box. I'm not sure why we did that, but that's what this line of folks looked like to me. Everyone was smashed in and ready to run!

Some folks, like my mister, were on horses, some were in wagons, a few were on bicycles, and a whole bunch of them were going to race around on foot! My mister was in the front on his fastest horse, but my missus wasn't far behind him in the wagon. She was going to drive that wagon as fast as she could, and we had to go with her! She made sure that we were tied good and tight to the back so we couldn't fall off. I was starting to get nervous by this time and was starting to think that being an immigrant wasn't the best idea.

While we were waiting for the start I overheard my mister reviewing the plan with my missus. He had found a lovely spot in a small valley with a creek and some trees, but it was so nice that he feared some others would get there before him. He said that while he was sneaking around at night he saw a lot of rule breakers already out there claiming homesteads when the race hadn't even begun yet. Folks had taken to calling them "Sooners" because they were out there sooner than they were supposed to be. He told my missus to make sure we followed behind him as close as we could, and stick to the plan once we got there.

Right about then, an eerie quiet came over the line, and I realized it was almost time to go. Then, we heard the sound of a bugle and off we went! We almost ran over some poor shlub who was racing on foot and ran right in front of us. Another wagon was so close behind us that the horse's spit was hitting me right in the face. So, not pleasant. Clouds of dust made it hard to breathe, and the ride was so bumpy that I felt for sure that we were going to bump clean off the back and all the wagons would run over us until we were mushier than a rotten roly-poly.

I glanced to the front of the wagon and saw my missus whipping the reins up and down and hollering at the horses to go faster. Her bonnet flew off her head and over our crate, finally plastering itself right over that slobbery horse's eyes. Serves him right.

We kept going mile after mile. The crowd began to thin out a bit as folks fanned off in all directions, but there were still quite a few heading toward the trees in front of us. My missus never let up on the speed, and I felt the wagon making a turn so fast that one side of the wagon lifted off the ground and we were rolling through the dirt on two wheels!

I twisted around to see where we were going, and just then, we hit a rock and the whole wagon flew up off the ground! Chickens aren't good flyers, and guess what, neither are wagons. When we hit the ground one of the back wheels smashed into a million pieces and we almost tipped over on our side! If you think we took that quietly, you're crazy! When we finally skidded to a stop I could just see my mister on the edge of the trees out in front of us. My missus leaped off the wagon bench and ran back to get us. She untied our crate quickly and dropped it on the ground, then she grabbed a bunch of long poles out of the wagon bed, and with the poles tucked under her arm on one side, she grabbed the edge of our crate with her other hand and started dragging us across the prairie.

Her hair had come undone and was flying around everywhere, and she was covered in dust. She had this wild look in her eyes. Like a crazy person. Of course, I couldn't see her well. I was doing my best to keep my footing as that crate bumped over rocks and prairie dog holes. I heard her yelp in pain when our crate hit the back of her heel, but nothing stopped her. She was hollering at our mister. I could see him more clearly by now, up ahead yelling at another mister who was waving a stick at him. Our crate was starting to splinter and I could tell my missus was getting tired because she was breathing hard. But she had a determined look on her face, and I knew she wasn't going back to the vegetable store if she could help it.

Then, she turned her ankle on a rock and fell down hard. She stayed down for a few seconds, until she shot up, ran to the back of our crate, opened up the door, and began screeching at the top of her voice, "HERE CHICKIE CHICKIE!"

Now where I come from "here chickie chickie" means treats and I know to come in a hurry when there are treats involved. So my missus took off, half limping, half running, dragging those poles and yelling, "HERE CHICKIE CHICKIE" with us running and flapping right behind her, feathers flying.

We must have been a sight to see. When we reached our mister, he was still yelling at the other mister so my missus quickly leaned those poles up tall against each other, then she whipped off her apron and tossed it over the top so it looked somewhat like a teepee. Then she plopped down in the dirt under her teepee, reached in her pocket, and threw us some pieces of mashed-up bread. I grabbed a piece of bread, but I was so tired from our sprint across the prairie, and so parched from my throat being full of dust, that I could hardly swallow it.

Now I could see another mister approaching us on a horse. He was dressed like a soldier and wanted to see what all the fuss was about. When he got there my mister explained to him that we got there first. Then, the other mister said no, he got there first. Since that Sooner didn't have a horse with him, and my mister was standing there next to his exhausted, panting horse, the soldier asked that Sooner if he outran my mister on foot. That Sooner looked the soldier in the eye and replied that he was an exceptionally fast runner. Then, the soldier looked over at us and asked whose chickens those were, when my mister said the chickens and the missus were all his, the soldier nodded and agreed that since we had a shelter and some livestock, this must be our land. That's when he sent that Sooner hightailing it back to town.

So, that's how we got our 160 acres in Oklahoma Territory for free. It's been over a year now, and my mister and missus have a proper house, and we have a proper chicken coop right next door.

I like being close to them even though it's gotten noisy over there since my missus got herself a baby. I don't mind though. I've been sitting on eggs myself, and I know it's getting time for them to hatch because I can feel the eggs moving underneath me. I like to cluck really low and soft at them so they will know that I'm waiting for them and they will be safe with me when they get here. My chicks won't be immigrants like me. They will live here in this valley, under the trees and by the creek for always.

The best part of all is that before my missus got her baby, she planted a vegetable garden right outside our coop. I've got my eyes on some green tomatoes that should be good and squishy right about the time my chicks are old enough for a treat. Maybe being an immigrant isn't so bad after all.

Fort Yellowstone, Wyoming 1896

Fort Yellowstone is a great place for a chicken like me to live on account of the fact that the animals in the park are protected and can't be killed or eaten. I'm pretty sure that rule applies to chickens too. Actually, maybe it doesn't apply to chickens. Maybe it just applies to wildlife? Although, chickens can live pretty wild lives at times. It probably does apply to us too, at least I hope so....

I've lived here at the fort for over a year now, and I'm enjoying it even though it does get pretty cold in the winter. We provide eggs for the fort cook to use in the big meals he makes for all the soldiers who are stationed here. The soldiers live out here so they can protect our nation's first national park. Being a national park means folks can't build railroads here or chop down trees or hunt animals and chickens. The soldiers make sure this place will be special for years to come. It's the first time our nation has decided to make a park, and I like being a part of history.

Yellowstone was chosen to be the first national park on account of all the crazy stuff going on around here. Sure, there are lots of nice mountains and rivers, but I've heard the soldiers tell stories about things I have a hard time believing. I overheard some soldiers talking, and one of them said he saw steaming pools of boiling water that will turn you into chicken soup in a second if you fall in!

Another said there's a hole in the ground that spits water into the sky almost every hour all day long! I'm not sure why the ground does that. Chickens don't really spit. We've been known to drool, but never spit. Then, I heard one mister talk about a place in the park where all the water smells like rotten eggs. I know what that smells like. Sometimes chickens like to find a secret place to lay eggs and hide them away and then we forget where we hid them. Last spring, a hen laid about twenty eggs out behind the woodpile and forgot all about them. Then, last week when the cook went back to get firewood, he stepped on the eggs, and boy howdy, did it smell bad! I'm not sure why the park wants to protect the pool that smells like rotten eggs, but they do.

When you think about it, it's pretty nice that we made a park in a place that is a mix of different types of things. Just because something's different, doesn't mean it's bad. I know what it's like to be different. I'm a type of chicken called a Polish. I have a poof on my head. It's such a big poof that the feathers flop over the top of my head, and you can't see my eyes most of the time. I can't see that great through my poofy feathers, and sometimes I bump into things.

Cook bought me at a town fair because he thought my poof would make the soldiers laugh. The soldiers get lonely sometimes, and laughing helps them feel better. So, I'm the entertainment a lot of the time. I don't mind. What makes me different makes me special.

When the soldiers aren't laughing at me or eating Cook's meals, they're out wandering around the park checking on things. That's how they caught the man who was killing bison and keeping their heads to take home with him. He thought folks back east would pay him money for those heads so they could hang them on their walls. Why would anyone want to hang a dead animal's head on the wall? That's kind of weird if you ask me.

When I heard about all that, I was concerned because if that man knew I was here, he would probably forget all about bison and try to take my head home with him since I'm way more interesting to look at than a smelly, old bison. I bet lots of folks back east hang chicken heads on their walls, especially poofy-headed chickens. But I didn't need to worry about that hunter because the soldiers caught him and took him to the jail here at the fort. When the folks far away heard about the bison heads, they decided to make that law about protecting the animals in the park. So I guess that bison head collector did me a favor because I'm pretty sure that I'm protected by law, even though I am a chicken.

You might be wondering how the soldiers wander around in the winter checking on things when the snow is really deep. Well, the soldiers walk around on something called snowshoes, and I think they got the idea for those shoes from looking at chicken feet. Those shoes are really wide so the soldiers don't sink down into the snow. Chicken feet have toes that are spread out. The same as a snowshoe. We walk on top of the snow and don't sink into it. I think they should call those shoes "chickenshoes" instead of snowshoes on account of the fact that we were the inspiration for them.

Another thing the soldiers like to do in the wintertime here is have big celebrations called holidays. The cook makes special meals for the soldiers to eat, and they end up singing songs and talking about their home folks and how much they miss them. Just last week they had a celebration that they called Thanksgiving, and us chickens had to lay as many eggs as we could so the cook could bake about a million cakes and pies for the celebration.

After the soldiers ate, we got our own celebration. Cook saved all the plate scrapings for us and we sure enjoyed all that good food. I noticed that he also saved leftovers for the pigs and goats to have some, so all of the barn animals got to enjoy some Thanksgiving too. The only ones who missed out were the turkeys. I didn't see them around. They must have been scratching around behind the barn. Come to think of it, I haven't seen them in a while.

I haven't thought much about them since they are an irritating lot, and so dumb! There is nothing dumber than a turkey. In fact, if it's raining outside, you have to chase the turkeys into the coop because they'll drown. That's how dumb they are. Now that I think of it, it rained a lot the week before the Thanksgiving celebration. That's probably what happened to that flock of turkeys. They probably drowned in the rain and that's why they weren't around to get the celebration leftovers. Oh well, more pumpkin pie for me.

My life in Yellowstone National Park is something I'm very proud of. Lots of times, folks stop by the fort on their way to look at the spitting hole in the ground and the smelly pools. They're excited to see all the crazy stuff this park has going on. I know from experience that being a bit different from the rest is not a bad thing. It's because this place is different that folks like it so much. Maybe that's why our nation decided to make it a park. To show that being different isn't a bad thing. It's a special thing. Perhaps our cook can have a celebration for this place and make a big meal, and all the soldiers can talk about what they like best about the park. Too bad those turkeys aren't around, I guess they'll miss that celebration too...

Robbers Roost, Utah 1900

I used to be an outlaw. Most chickens live quiet lives and are up-standing members of their flock, but not me. Being an outlaw is not something I ever thought about being when I was young. Like most outlaws, I kind of stumbled into it, or rather, was shoved into a sack and tossed into it.

For the first couple of years of my life, I lived peacefully behind a general store in Hanksville, Utah. Hanksville was a brand new town at the time, and folks needed chickens so they could have eggs for breakfast. It was the job of us chickens to lay as many eggs as possible so my missus could sell them in her store. I was a particular favorite of my missus due to the fact that I liked to lay an egg a day. Most hens lay an egg every other day, but not me. Laying eggs was my thing, and I was good at it. My missus was so impressed with me that she would often bring me little treats, like half a biscuit or a piece of boiled potato.

Back to how I ended up an outlaw. It happened quite by accident. My missus used to employ a town girl to work in the shop in the afternoon so she could be home when her younguns got home from school. One day, some nice-looking men came into the store wanting to buy some provisions for a camp they were starting. Well, that town girl was what my missus used to call "boy crazy," and she was so smitten with one of those misters that she would have done just about anything for him. So when he asked if she had any full-grown laying chickens for sale, she walked out in the back of the store, nabbed me and a couple of other hens, tossed us in a burlap sack, and gave us to that mister.

Those men who were asking for chickens weren't exactly strangers. Everyone around town knew them. They did a lot of business in our town, and I guess that's why folks didn't mind that they were outlaws. Their leader was named Butch Cassidy, and he was a polite and friendly mister who treated the ladies with special attention. Folks called him charming. I'm not sure what that means since chickens aren't charming, but lots of folks thought Butch and his gang were great. So when they tied that burlap sack to the horn of a saddle, I was disappointed to leave my comfortable life but not nervous to go off and live with Butch and the boys. After a long, bumpy ride, I began my life as an outlaw at Robbers Roost.

At first, I missed my life behind the store, and I worried my missus was missing me, but eventually, I grew to enjoy how quiet it was. Even though it's called Robbers Roost, it isn't like a chicken roost at all. There aren't a lot of trees to roost in. Just a lot of red cliffs and canyons. There isn't much to the camp, just a few cabins, a horse barn, and a corral for all the donated cattle and horses. My misters are always bringing cattle and horses up here to put in the corral. When someone brings some in, they always yell something like, "Look boys what I got for us! How's that for a donation?"

Then they would all laugh. I think folks are pretty generous to give away so many cows and horses. My misters bring them here to our hideaway because some folks might forget they gave them away and want them back. This way they won't know where to look for them, and my misters can keep them. So, this is a good and quiet place to live. My only complaint is that I wish there were more grasshoppers, but you can't have everything.

Most of the time, it's just us livestock and One-Eyed Pete who live here. One-Eyed Pete is the mister who takes care of this place when the other misters are all out rounding up donations. I once knew a rooster who had only one eye. He lost an eye in a fight and for the rest of his life, he had to turn his whole head around if he wanted to see what was going on on the other side. One-Eyed Pete didn't have to do that though, folks have their eyes on the front of their faces, not the sides of their heads like chickens do.

It's not always lonely around here though. Plenty of misters ride through looking for a place to hide out for a spell or just needing a place to sleep for the night. Robbers Roost is pretty famous amongst the outlaw crowd. My favorite times are when Butch and his friends come through. He calls them "The Wild Bunch," but I don't know why, they don't seem too wild to me.

They're fun to have around. They mostly like to laugh, play cards, and practice shooting their guns. When they aren't busy with all that, they like to plan their next trip. They like to go on trips and mostly talk about visiting banks and trains. It must be great to get to see so many interesting banks and railroads! All that planning makes them thirsty, so they like to drink a lot. For the longest time, I thought their lives were nothing but adventure and good times. It took a particular visitor to make me change my mind about enjoying being an outlaw.

One time, all the misters except One-Eyed Pete were off on a trip, and an outlaw came through all on his lonesome. It wasn't unusual to have an outlaw stop for a night, but as I found out later, this man wasn't an outlaw at all. He said his name was Lee Roy Davis, and he was looking for Butch and the rest of the boys. One-Eyed Pete was a bit suspicious of him since he had never heard of him before.

During his conversation with One-Eyed Pete, Lee Roy started talking about some of the Wild Bunch and how they had not only robbed folks but had killed lawmen and bystanders in the towns they visited. He talked about how there were children without a father or a mother now because of what the Wild Bunch did. Well, that bothered my heart because I had a brood of chicks at the time, and it made me recollect a time when One-Eyed Pete ran out of corn for us chickens to have for our breakfast. He didn't like to make the long trip into town unless he absolutely had to. He was lazy like that.

He told us to just go out and find our own food. I wouldn't have minded so much, but my chicks needed something to eat and bugs were scarce in those canyons. Well, by some miracle I actually caught myself a small frog. Frogs are good eating if they're small enough to handle. I had a half dozen chicks. That's a lot of beaks to feed, so I was grateful for that frog. But before we could get started eating, another chicken sprinted in and stole that frog right away from us. By the time I realized what had happened and put up a chase, that chicken had disappeared. You know what she did? She hid. She hid away and ate that whole frog all by herself. And that's when I realized that's what we were all doing at Robbers Roost. We were hiding.

I began to think that even though Butch and the boys seemed like fun-loving, nice misters, they were really bad men who did things so bad that they had to hide out here far away from everyone. It occurred to me that maybe all those donated horses and cows weren't donations after all. They didn't get those horses and cows from rich folks. They got them from regular folks who were just farmers trying to scratch out a living for themselves and their families. Just like I was trying to do. That's when I started regretting being an outlaw chicken.

I heard some time later that Lee Roy Davis was really a Pinkerton Detective named Charley Siringo who was just pretending to be an outlaw so he could catch up with the Wild Bunch and take them to jail. I didn't know how to feel about that. I liked my outlaw friends. I just didn't like what they did. But anyone can change, can't they?

I have hope that Butch and the boys will change their ways. That's why I was encouraged when I heard that Butch and a friend they called Sundance, hightailed it down to South America. That made me happy. I didn't want Butch to go to jail. I just wanted him to change his ways and stop stealing from folks. This was Butch's chance to have a new start. I sure hope he reforms himself and has a great time in South America!

Cripple Creek, Colorado 1896

M y mister is a doctor. In fact, that's how I came to live here in town. While my mister was out visiting a missus who lived out on a homestead, she decided to have a baby. Why folks don't just hatch out their babies like chickens do, I'll never know. At any rate, that family couldn't afford to pay, so they gave me to the doctor as payment. That was fine with me. I have always wanted to be a town chicken. The doctor brought me here, and I joined his flock of assorted chickens, ducks, geese, and even a goat that were all given as payment for services. By the way, no one likes the goat. All he does is make a lot of noise and eat all the grass.

We used to live in a shed behind a saloon. My mister lived in the saloon. He had a couple of rooms at the back where he did his doctoring and his sleeping. It's a good thing he had his office in the saloon because folks who spend the evening in the saloon usually end up needing a doctor by the time the night's over. It's my understanding that misters go to a saloon to have a good time, but why having a good time means you end up with a broken nose or a busted rib is a mystery to me. For us chickens, a good time means a belly full of grasshoppers. Maybe folks should be more like chickens when they want to have a good time. But then, my mister wouldn't have a job and the world would probably run out of grasshoppers.

I'm proud to live with my mister, he does a lot to help people. Cripple Creek is a mining town, and folks spend most of their time underground. There was this one time when there was a terrible accident down in the mine. Some rocks slid right down and trapped a miner when his leg got stuck under the rocks. Well, my mister grabbed his doctor bag and went almost 500 feet down into that mine to help. He was down there a long time, and I started to get a little curious. So me and another hen wandered over to the mine entrance and joined the crowd. It took some time, but eventually, they brought that miner up on a stretcher. I was surprised to see he left one of his legs in the mine! My mister came up with him and everyone clapped for him and slapped him on the back for saving that miner's life.

When I thought about that miner and his missing leg, it was a puzzlement for me. One time, I hurt my toe something awful, and I had to stand around on one leg most of the day to keep the pain away. The standing wasn't a problem. It was when I had to get from one place to another on only one leg that was hard. I had to just grit my beak and walk on my bad toe to catch a beetle or get a drink.

Now that poor miner doesn't even have a bad leg to walk on, so I don't know how he is going to get from here to there on just one leg. Plus, I can't help wondering, did they just leave his leg down in the mine?

I'm hoping I can live with my mister for always, but one day I got myself into some trouble that I thought might make my mister send me away. Lucky for me I was able to focus the blame on someone else. You see, sometimes sick folk stay overnight in the doctor's office in the back of the saloon. My mister likes to keep an eye on them and give them medicine at night when they need it. Well, after a couple of misters got in a shootout on the street in front of the saloon, one of them had to come and sleep in the office because he got a bullet shot clean through him and out the other side.

He was OK at first, but then his bullet wound got infected and he was terrible sick. My mister was worried he would die. I don't know what it means to die because that's something folks do, not chickens, but from the way everyone was acting, I guessed it was not a great thing. One afternoon I decided to check on that man, so I jumped up on the window sill to look into the window and see how he was doing. You won't believe what I saw! That sick mister was sleeping on the bed and you could see the bullet wound on his side plain as day, but the shocking thing was that there were these big fatty worms all over it! I don't know what those worms were doing and I don't care, I just couldn't believe such fat, tasty worms were behind that window glass and just out of my reach!

That night I dreamed about those worms, so the next day I hid under the porch and I overheard my mister talking. I heard him call those worms "leeches," and he told a missus who was helping him that he was expecting a new shipment of them coming in on the noon stage. Well, that was almost too much for me to handle. If my mister was expecting a whole box of those worms to come riding in on the stage I absolutely had to get me some of them.

I promised myself that I would only get two or three and leave plenty of them behind for the sick mister to have. But I knew getting my beak on them wouldn't be easy, so I made a plan. I lurked on the side of the saloon until I saw my mister walking down the street with his box of tasty leeches from the stage. Then, I ran over to that worthless goat and gave him a tremendous peck right on his rear.

Well, that made him so mad he started chasing me all around the yard, and I led him right up to the back door where my mister was about to grab the handle and go in. I ran right between my mister's legs, and that goat followed me and smacked right into my mister. That goat hit him so hard that my mister's legs went flying up in the air and my mister ended up landing flat on his back in the dirt! The box went flying and hit the ground hard, breaking open and spilling glass and leaches everywhere. I felt bad about my mister falling so hard on his back. I had forgotten that folks don't have wings that they can flap and help them have a softer landing. But when I saw those fat leeches squiggling around in the dust, I just couldn't help myself. I ran over and grabbed one and took off with it!

My mister sat up, and I was glad to see that he wasn't hurt too bad. But boy was he mad at that goat! After he gathered up the leeches and dusted them off a bit, he got the saloon bartender to help him, and they caught that goat and took him away. I suppose I should feel bad about that because, after all, it was all my plan that made it happen. But like I said, no one liked that goat anyway.

You may think that I kept dreaming of how to get my beak on some more of those leeches and you're right. The only thing that stopped me was a few days after the goat incident, our whole street burned to the ground in a city fire. We all got out safe. All of us except the leeches. Now my mister has his new office in a proper storefront on the other side of Cripple Creek. He even has his name on the door and everything.

He says that he's glad he isn't working out of the back of a saloon anymore. He says that times are changing and he has to adapt to new ways. I agree with him, but I can't help but wonder about those leeches. Did they burn up all the way or did they just get a bit toasty? I'm sorry I never got a chance to scratch around in the ashes. Bar-be-que leeches sound mighty tasty to me.

Cheyenne, Wyoming, 1904

I once heard someone say that if you're running around acting frantic, then you're acting like a "chicken with its head cut off." Well, even though I think that's a pretty insensitive thing to say, I do think that's the way the whole town is acting this week. Everyone is busy because this week is the annual Cheyenne Frontier Days.

That's when folks come in on the train from all over the place to watch the cowboys wrestle with the cattle. Our town started Frontier Days because we heard of this town in Colorado that had something called the Potato Day Festival where I guess they wrestled potatoes. Since we grow cows and not potatoes in these parts, I don't rightly know how potatoes act and how you go about wrestling one. I'm glad that town in Colorado didn't have a Chicken Day Festival. I wouldn't want folks around here to get any ideas.

There's a lot more to see at the Frontier Days than just steer wrestling. There's also a contest for horses to try and buck off a cowboy. The horse that does the best job wins a blue ribbon. The cowboy usually takes that horse's ribbon for himself, which isn't very nice if you ask me. Then there's another contest where cowboys ride around, and when they see a cow just minding its own business and not bothering anyone, they jump off their horse, grab that cow, and tie it up around his feet. I'm pretty sure that this is a humiliating experience for the cow.

In addition to the regular cowboys, there's also a whole lot of crazy folks who perform shows here. There's one mister who is confused about how to ride a horse and he rides his horse by hanging upside down and holding on to the horse's belly. Talk about dumb! Then, there's a lady who thinks you're supposed to stand up on the saddle and ride that way. I guess she does it so she won't have a sore backside when she has to go on long rides. All of this is pretty entertaining for the folks from the East who travel out here for Frontier Days, but there's one cowboy in particular who puts on a show no one could ever forget.

His name is Bill Pickett, and he's pretty famous for all his riding and roping tricks. He's been at it his whole life. But the trick he's been doing this week has got everyone talking. He calls it "bulldogging" and folks are pretty amazed when they see him jump on a cow and drag it to the ground by biting on its upper lip. What most folks don't know is that he got the idea from me.

A couple of years ago, Bill came into Cheyenne on a cattle drive before the Frontier Days became the big deal they are today. He was quite popular since he already had a reputation for being a cowboy who could do tricks, so folks were always buying him drinks and wanting to hear his stories. Well, one afternoon I was out behind the saloon with a few of my hens scratching around and having a restful afternoon. Bill Pickett and some other misters came out the back door of the saloon and decided to do their drinking out under a shade tree.

One of them picked up some rocks and started chunking them at me. That got my hackles up. I'm a peaceable rooster most of the time, but if someone treats me unfairly, I can get ornery. I held it together and just let out some warning cackles, but when he started smacking some of my hens with rocks I just couldn't stand for that. I ran over to him and jumped at him with my spurs out. That rock chunker was able to deflect my first attack, so I started pacing and putting up a fuss, waiting for another chance to strike. That chance came quicker than I thought when he stooped down to pick up some more rocks.

That's when I leaped up and instead of spurring him, I attacked his face with my beak and latched on to his upper lip. He let out a screech and started batting at me with his hands to get me to let go, but I hung on tight and started spurring on him with my super sharp spurs. Since I was also flapping my wings like crazy, he couldn't see where he was going and he backed up and tripped over a tree root and fell straight to the ground, which is where he stayed, feebly batting at me and trying to get me to let go. Bill and his friends were laughing and hooting at this like it was part of the Frontier Days show. Since I had made my point, I let go and strutted back to my hens. I let out a triumphant crow or two, then we headed down the alley and back toward our coop.

That was two years ago, and it didn't surprise me at all the other day when I was walking past the telegraph office with my girls on our way to the cemetery to scratch around for bugs, and we overheard some folks talking about Bill Picket and his bulldogging. Apparently, he took that trick he learned from me and used it on some cows. He just wrestles a cow to the ground by biting its upper lip. Of course, Bill doesn't have spurs like me so he has to make sure to bite pretty hard. The cow is so outraged by this treatment that it just lays in the dirt in shock until Bill lets go. The crowd goes wild for this. They like it even better than the man who rides upside down. You just can't understand some folks.

It doesn't bother me that Bill stole my trick. I wouldn't want to be a Frontier Day performer anyway. What a waste of time. I'm way too busy taking care of my flock and hunting for tasty bugs for us to eat. So, my hens and I will stick to the cemetery this week where it's nice and quiet. There are plenty of bugs there for us to get and no wrestling is necessary. I know enough to stay out of the way of all the town shenanigans during Frontier Days week. After all, this isn't my first rodeo.

Beatrice, Nebraska, 1877

Grasshoppers are pretty tasty, and since there are about a million of them around, that's what I eat mostly. But lately, something unusual has happened. All over the ground, there are small pieces of green sprouting up. I tasted some the other day, and they're pretty good too! My missus says that it's called "grass." I have never seen grass before because I was hatched last year during the grasshopper plague, and those grasshoppers ate every blade of grass before it was even out of the dirt.

My missus says that even though there are still a lot of grasshoppers around these days, a late snowstorm killed most of the hatching ones off, so that's why we have grass growing now. I'm glad for it. A grasshopper with some grass on the side is a pretty good meal if you ask me.

My missus is what they call a "homesteader." Some folks call her a "sodbuster," but she doesn't much like that name. She came here almost ten years ago when the boys were still younguns. Now they're older and they work as hard as any man around these parts. My missus came to get land, and all she had to do was live here and make it a nice place to live, then the land was free. Her folks back home said she was crazy to haul her young boys out to the prairie and prove up a piece of land without a mister, but she was determined. Her mister died in a civil war but she wasn't going to let that stop her from following what she and her mister had always dreamed of- owning their own farm.

In case you're wondering what a civil war is, it's kind of like a rooster fight. Except, instead of being just the two roosters who fight, the rest of the flock all start fighting each other too. That sounds pretty terrible to me. I hope we never have a civil war in our hen house.

Life has been very pleasant here lately, partly due to winter being over and partly due to Edward coming back. Edward is the oldest of the missus' younguns. When the grasshoppers came three years ago, she sent him away with the cows to her brother's farm in Idaho. The grasshoppers ate up all the cow's food so they would have died if she hadn't sent them away. I suppose those cows could have eaten the grasshoppers like us chickens do, but cows must not think grasshoppers are good eatin' because they wouldn't touch them. She sent Edward away with eleven cows, and he came back with fourteen cows due to several of them having calves while they were away. She says they can sell some of the cows and buy the homestead next to ours since the Flannerys had to give up and go back home when the grasshoppers ate everything. The only reason my missus didn't have to give up and go back home was because her home folks sent her packages with food and other things to help her out. Now that we have all these cows, she will have the money to buy lots of seed to plant the crops. I hope those grasshoppers stay away. I don't have a home to go back to. This is my home.

Edward is excited to buy the neighbor's farm. While he was away, he met a young missus that he wants to bring here to live. That makes my missus very happy. She says when Edward marries his missus, her family will grow. Family is something I have a hard time understanding since chickens don't have families. During the long years that Edward was away, my missus was sad and lonely for him to come home.

I remember when I was hatched, I loved my mother, but something strange happened a couple of months after I was born. I stopped thinking of her as my mother, and she stopped wanting to be with us chicks all the time. I wasn't sad about it. It was just the way of things. When I saw my missus cry for Edward, I thought it must be nice to want someone with you for always.

After we have a good crop this year, my missus says we can build a real house and stop living in the ground like gophers. I don't know why she wants a real house. I think gophers must be the smartest folks around because our dug-out house is warm in the winter and cool in the summer. It's dug right into the side of a hill. My missus and the boys live in one part and us chickens have our very own part with our own door and everything.

One of the best parts is that because the walls are made of dirt, sometimes worms or bugs squirm through the dirt and fall out of the walls. It's like having a snack without ever having to work for it! I'm not sure why the missus doesn't like it when that happens in her part of our dugout. Us chickens think it's the best part!

Life on the prairie has been hard for my missus. She gets out into the fields with the plow just like the boys, and she spends all the rest of her time cooking and cleaning and washing and planting.

She always says it is all worth it to make a better life for her children and the grandchildren she will have someday.

Even though she's so tired all the time, she always smiles at the boys when they come in to supper and tries to hide her tiredness from them. She's also very quick to go and help a neighbor, no matter how tired she is. Though she hides her true feelings from everyone around her, I know her best. I know her because I always go with her to the garden in the evenings when she goes to sit on the rock.

The rock is a big boulder on the edge of her vegetable garden. While I scratch around looking for a beetle, she sits on the rock and talks to a friend of hers named Jesus. I have never seen him. He must stay behind the sod barn and listen from there. She talks to him and tells him what she is grateful for and what she is wishing for. Sometimes she quietly sings a song to him, and she always has tears in her eyes when she sings.

According to the song, there was something called "amazing grace" that Jesus used to help my missus back when she used to be lost and blind. I know what both of those things feel like. One time I chased a grasshopper so far that when I looked up, all I could see all around me was tall grass, and I didn't know how to get home. That was pretty scary for me until I heard the rooster crow in the distance. That's how I knew which direction to go to get home.

And as for being blind, every night when the sun goes down, us chickens are blind. We don't have a light in our coop, but I'm not scared. I hop up on the roost and get real close to the rooster. That way, I can lean into him and I'm not alone in the dark anymore. So, I know how nice it is to have someone to lean on when I need It most.

Sometimes, instead of singing, she asks him what she should do about a sick horse or a broken plow. Though I never hear him when he answers her, I know he does answer because a few days later, she will always thank him for helping her. That whole time Edward was gone she would always ask him to take care of Edward for her, and now Edward is home safe, so I guess Jesus is the best friend a person could ever have.

Those evenings at the rock are my favorite time of the day. Most of the other hens have already made their way back to our sod hen house, but I always stay out to be with my missus because I love to hear her sing. Chickens sing too. Mostly after we have laid an egg. It's not a pretty song though. Nothing like the songs my missus sings. Even though my missus' life is hard and she is bone tired, after she spends time sitting on that rock, she always has a small smile on her face. Like she has the strength to face another day. I think her smile helps her boys feel strengthened too. I know it helps me to feel like everything is good in the world.

After our time at the rock, she makes a clicking sound to me with her tongue, and I follow her back to our sod house. She smiles at me and says goodnight to all the other hens as she shuts our door tight so we will be safe in the night. Then, I hear her go into her house next door, speak softly to her boys, and shut her door tight. From listening to her at the rock, I know that she believes that whatever dangers, toils, and snares may come, amazing grace will always lead her home.

THE END

ABOUT THE AUTHOR

Arlene Davenport traded a life of battling traffic in the big city for a life of watching the sunset in rural Texas. When she's not teaching junior high English, she spends her time reading, writing, gardening, and trying to survive the Texas heat. She lives in a small town south of Austin with her husband, two dogs, a cat, and fourteen chickens.

Printed in Great Britain
by Amazon

43406031R00076